NINE WOMEN

TONY TEDESCHI

Also by Tony Tedeschi

Unfinished Business

A complex thriller set in the cutthroat world of corporate
maneuvering . . .
Raymond Chandleresque . . .

- Kirkus Reviews

From a massacre in a Honduran village to major corporate
boardrooms where greed reigns, "Unfinished Business" grips
you from the first page and doesn't let go until the stunning
conclusion. A provocative insightful thriller.

- Donald Bain
Murder, She Wrote Books

The Whitford Way

The story of the human side of building a great business.
Whether you're a high school teacher, a surgeon, or Harvard's
newest MBA, this is definitely worth reading.

- Joseph J. Dunn
After 100 Years: Corporate Profits, Wealth & American Society

Live Via Satellite

The time was ripe and the concept was inevitable; it was
certainly bobbing around in the back of many ingenious minds.

- Arthur C. Clarke, 2001, A Space Odyssey

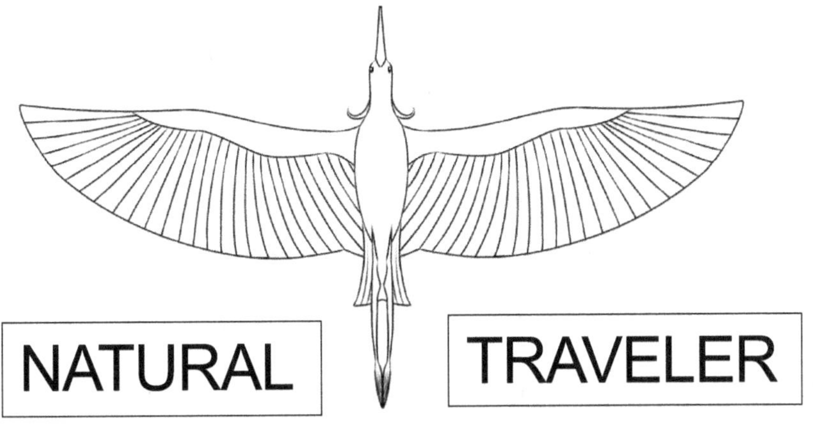

NATURAL TRAVELER

BOOKS®

*The
Great White Heron,
symbol for those of us
bound to wade
into the marshes
of life's journey,
and never give up.*

For information, contact:
Natural Traveler Books
Natural Traveler LLC
5 Brewster Street, Unit 2, No. 204
Glen Cove, NY 11542.

This is a work of fiction. Names, characters, places and incidents are used fictitiously. Any resemblances to any persons, living or dead, or any corporate entities, are entirely coincidental.

ISBN: 979-8-9878830-1-3

Original artwork by

Sharafina binti Teh Sharifuddin

FOR

CANDY

CONTENTS

BY TONY TEDESCHI

I have been keeping journals and writing in notebooks since I wrote my first stories, in my first notebook, in my early teenage years. That early compulsion to write morphed into a profession after a degree in journalism and a masters in English Lit. I've spent most of my adult life as a freelance writer, crafting articles for magazines and newspapers, writing business books and eventually a novel. Lately, I have been composing the music and writing the book for a musical play in partnership with a talented director. It's a disease. You catch it; there is no cure.

There have been times, after I'd submitted an article, when I was drawn back to my notes because while writing them I couldn't turn loose of the question, "what if?" What if the subject had acted differently, had confronted a situation or situations, which were more complex, compelling or conflicting than what had actually happened? I have journals and notebooks filled with many of those what-ifs, generated by encounters with people during a lifetime traveling the world.

Along the way, these creative gymnastics spawned possible plotlines for my short stories. Not only had all this become a matter of process, but the process itself has become a plot device, as in these nine stories, with my alter ego, Michael Rhodes.

In this collection, he has taken me into a parallel universe of his own making, in his quest for . . .

Well, start turning pages and he'll take you there, as well.

Introduction

The two women outside the window of the coffee bar in Soho had attracted my attention. One of them in particular. They were in a syncopated conversation, attentive dialogue alternating with more-animated moments. The scene was distracting me from my notetaking. A non-drama with no discernible reason to give it more than passing attention.

Yet . . .

I was sitting on a stool at a tall, rectangular table placed directly up against the large picture window. It was the early '70s. I was in Soho to do an article about the neighborhood during its repurposing as an art and music center, just south of Manhattan's already long-established artsy center of Greenwich Village on Soho's northern border.

Watching the dialog on the other side of the window, I began an almost frenzied need to scribble down my thoughts about one of the two women who'd taken my attention away from my work, despite my knowing nothing more about her than her surface features, clothing choices, facial gestures and arm movements. Nonetheless, an entire history for her was flowing from my pen onto the pages of my notebook.

At the conclusion of their conversation, the two women parted company. The one I'd been writing about headed for the door to the coffee bar. Once inside, she surveyed the room, well-occupied by the mid-morning coffee break crowd, which had taken up some or all of the seats at all the tables around the main portion of the room. She headed for the empty stool next to mine.

"May I?" she asked.

"Of course," I answered.

She draped her jacket over the back of the stool, smiled at me and said, "don't let anyone sit here while I'm off to get my coffee."

"I'll guard it with my life," I replied, watching her movements and scribbling more notes about her, until she started heading back. I closed my notebook and dropped it into my backpack.

"Watcha writing about?" she asked, as she took her seat. "I could see you writing vigorously, while I was with my friend outside."

"Really," I said. "I wouldn't think you'd notice something like that from afar, through a window, no less, especially when engaged in what looked like a compelling conversation."

"I'm a very attentive person," she replied. "I notice what's going on around me."

I studied her for a moment, then decided to take the risk. "I was writing about you," I said.

She blurted out a laugh. "No way."

"Way."

"But you don't know anything about me."

"I know what I could see. I'm a very attentive person."

"Touché," she said with a smile. "Can I read what you wrote?"

Of course, now, after baiting her like that, I had no choice but to let her. I retrieved my notebook from my backpack, opened it to where I'd been writing and handed it to her.

She went through a range of facial expressions as she read. When she'd finished, she told me I had gotten some of her very right, some of her partially right, a good deal of her wrong, even a bit very wrong.

I replied I'd likely gotten most of it right, because the person on the pages was not her, but a character in a possible story that might develop from what I'd written.

"Why me?" she asked. "Why in the world would I inspire anything like that from a distance, through a plate glass window, while having the kind of conversation that goes on all over a city like this?"

"You know," I replied, "I seldom know the answer to that. Something just clicks for me."

She seemed to study me for a moment, with a strange look of comprehension on her face. "Odd," she said, "I almost get it. Get what you're talking about."

I explained that as a writer, I was always alert to possible subjects for my stories. I told her that while this brief interaction between her and me might somehow follow some as-yet-undefined path, since I didn't know her name and would have no way of finding her, if what I'd written ever made it into print, her anonymity was fully protected.

"Well," she said, as we both finished our coffees and rose to leave, "I'm not likely to forget this meeting, at least not any time soon."

"The unexplained connections in life," I replied. "I . . ."

But my struggle to continue with the rest of a reply found no place else to go. What had happened here was petering out, losing all of its energy in the world of the real.

She just shook her head, and we went our separate ways.

My life has been more a journey over decades of traveling far and wide researching my articles, but always keenly aware of those subjects triggering biographies of characters, acting in settings of my parallel universe.

So, who among my female characters are real, partially real, mostly fictitious, complete figments of my imagination?

I was a student at MIT and belonged to a fraternity there. But did I ever meet anyone like Siobhan Leary in the opening story, *Chemistry*?

I did serve four years as an Air Force officer during the Vietnam War. But was anyone like Aldina, in the story, *Tumbleweed,* even a remote part of my experience there? Let alone a metaphor for the woman I'd marry?

I finished the New York City Marathon with a woman who was a policeman's wife, and I did have a neighbor with a severely disabled son. But were they one and the same person or a projection into the single character who becomes the love interest in *The Policeman's Wife.*

There was a Josephine, who was my friend in elementary school, and two other young girls in my neighborhood with whom I played as a very young boy, but . . .

Is even the encounter with the woman at the coffee bar in Soho real or imagined, as the central character in a story I said I might one day write? I'm not even sure if I remember an encounter like that well enough to answer my own question. It was a long time ago. But I did find five pages about such an experience in a long-forgotten notebook.

-- Michael Rhodes

In the distance, small islands seemed clumps of blue-gray clay in the mist that ran to the edges of the horizon. An overturned canoe languished in a patch of grass, its fiberglass underside growing a crystalline white crust in the heat of the sun. . . . . I closed my eyes, tried to empty my mind and conjoin with the natural environment. Then I felt it. The intrusion of her presence . . .

CHEMISTRY

Siobhan Leary met Joe Dalton, in the summer of 1959, at a dance in Williamsburg, Virginia, not far from her hometown on the Tidewater Peninsula. It was the summer after each had finished high school. Joe had crashed the party by tagging along with a friend whose family had moved to the area from Boston. He had spent the night before boozing in Manhattan with another expatriate Bostonian whose family had an apartment in a high-rise just north of Greenwich Village. Then Joe headed south the next morning in his brand new Ford Crown Victoria, a gift from his father, Joseph senior.

Joe was the latest in a long line of Boston Brahmins, who traced their ancestry back through congressmen and senators to a limb on the Adams family tree. His car could have been one of those nifty two-seaters, with the "gull-wing" doors, Mercedes had just introduced, had Joe acceded to his father's wishes and entered the pre-law program at Harvard, following in the footsteps of all the first sons before him. Instead, he chose a mechanical engineering major at MIT. Joe loved getting his hands greasy and he preferred the lines of the Ford – the bold chrome strip over the roof, the way the profile reminded him of a speedboat – no matter how pedestrian his father found both the car and his son's work-a-day choice of profession.

"MIT ain't too shabby," Joe had said to his father when he'd made his decision known to the old bastard.

"Isn't," the senior Dalton corrected.

Siobhan was the ideal accessory to Joe's diminution in family status. She was the daughter of Irish immigrants who ran a barely solvent bed-'n'-breakfast in the tiny hamlet of Providence Forge, catering to redneck hunters and fishermen, instead of the busloads of tourists who poured into nearby Colonial Williamsburg throughout the year. And she had just a trace of that Irish lilt to her voice, an accent the Anglo Bostonians would have found particularly grating.

I met Joe when we were both rushed by the same fraternity. I *had* acceded to my father's wishes that I become an engineer, despite the fact that all I ever wanted out of life was to write about the Yankees for the New York Daily News and to one day buy a used Crown Victoria. I especially cultivated, for me, the romantic notion of wandering about the sidelines during spring training in Florida, on those cold February days back in New York, when the dank, gray snows had encrusted to particularly unattractive icy formations, outside our apartment in Queens, New York, where, inside, on the black-and-white TV screen, late of a Saturday afternoon, the bright light I took to be from a sun the color of one of those Florida oranges was shafting across the late innings of a Florida ball diamond.

My father repaired TVs for a company called Play-Rite. The owner had gotten a two-year certificate as an electrical technician from a trade school in Manhattan. My father was a high school dropout who was smarter than the guy who ran the place, but did not have the credentials. He did, however, have something to crow about when first his son made the prestigious Brooklyn Technical High School, then graduated tenth in a class of fifteen hundred on his way to MIT. I liked giving my father something to crow about, because he was a really nice guy and he was very good to me. But, I did get him to accept that chemistry would be my particular scientific interest, not electricity.

Nonetheless, I immediately had problems with the curriculum. I was part of a group randomly selected for an experimental calculus class with which I was wrestling, and the rearrangement of the math curriculum seriously compromised my ability to do physics problems, which required the more traditional math I would not be studying until later in the semester. Furthermore, I found the more confusing problem/solutions of organic models far less to my liking than the inorganic chemistry I had aced in high school, largely because the latter followed far-fewer complex paths from A through B to C. I found my favorite freshman course was a catch-all the Institute called Humanities, a conglomeration of English Lit, Western Civ, Psychology, Philosophy, et al, added to the freshman curriculum so that MIT students would be able to engage in meaningful intellectual conversation in social situations with female students from other universities. I was acing the term papers in Humanities and loving that, doing poorly in just about everything else.

"Mike Rhodes, what the hell are you doing here?" Joe asked after I flunked the first of a string of freshman physics exams. "Let's face it, you ain't no chemist and this ain't no fucking place for a writer."

"Isn't," I countered with my chin in my shoes, "isn't no fucking place for a writer."

Joe was inexplicably drawn to me, despite the fact that I was never completely comfortable in his presence. I was intimidated by all that old family money, that waspy American last name. What do you want with me? I'd always wanted to ask. You're smarter than I am. You're so much richer than me. You know how to act in situations I have never even encountered. And you'll leave here to enter a life laid out before you, no matter how much you buck your old man. I was sure "fuck the buck of my old man" would be his answer, but I doubted he'd ever walk away from his inheritance. I was wrong. Siobhan had done him in. She batted the lashes above those emerald greens at him at the post-high school dance he'd crashed and he'd had no choice but to ask her to do the slow one that was playing. Once she'd pressed that incredible chest of hers to his and nestled that sweet-smelling cheek into the curve of his neck and shoulder, he'd been drawn into the first battle of a war he was destined to lose, complicated by the fact that he fell hopelessly in love with her, then and there.

Siobhan followed Joe north to Boston at the end of that summer and took a job waitressing at one of those beer-and-burger joints in Back Bay, where the waitresses dressed up like medieval wenches and spoke in bad attempts at cockney accents. (In her case, she just let her Irish accent play.) She was a big hit with the clientele, what with that great cleavage, that red hair, and that genuine accent. She never forgot the slightest nuance in an order and often had a quippy comment to make as she dropped a burger plate in front of a customer or slid a stein across the table. For lodgings, she hooked up with a couple of Boston U coeds who were waitressing for some mad money. The three of them took a furnished, one-bedroom apartment, with Siobhan opting for the sofa-bed in the living room rather than share the bedroom, which made it reasonably private when she brought Joe back with her, unless one of her roommates got up to pee when they were right in the middle of it.

Siobhan became a fixture at our Saturday night house parties, most of the time appended to Joe's right or left arm. Damn, she was a beauty with that raging red hair, those penetrating green, green eyes, that milk-white skin and that incredible bod. It was easy to see how any man would lust after her (I was sure a half-dozen rednecks-in-waiting put shotguns in their mouths and blew their heads off when she left southern Virginia for the center of the Yankee universe), but I was just as sure that Joe loved her, would have if she were not the least bit attractive. You could see it in his eyes whenever he looked at her. Hell, it was all over the look on his face whenever she spoke with that musical lilt. It was a connection thing with him. He told me, early on, that he saw her as one of those people who would throw herself at life and dance around in it. Something he had always wanted to do, while growing up in a family that lived simply to critique life. He felt Siobhan would show him how to live.

Me, I had mixed feelings about Siobhan. I could see that joie de vivre, which so captivated Joe, but I could also see that gleam in her eye, to which he was either oblivious or chose to ignore. It was hard to imagine her as a wife with little redheads tugging at her skirts, one of those raw-boned women, scrubbing clothes against a washboard like in those 1940s black-and-white movies set in Ireland. She had the gleam that never dies out.

As our freshman year drew to a close, I was completing an academic recovery, second semester, from a first semester that almost resulted in my flunking out. I hated the Institute. I hated the work. I really had loved chemistry in high school, when coming up with the right answers was more like winning at a quiz show. But now, I couldn't see myself behind a test tube for the rest of my life. I'd only agreed to stay on there after a dismal first semester because I did not want to devastate my father, so we agreed I would give it one more shot. It was more a matter of proving I could succeed at "The Toot," than a heightening level of interest in the subject matter. It merely delayed the inevitable.

Joe was wrestling his own problems, as well. His father was diagnosed with advanced colon cancer and was given but a short time to live, so Joe was spending every weekend at the family's manse in the Brookline suburb of Boston. Given the tension that arose after the family's first and only encounter with Siobhan, whom Joe had brought to dinner one night shortly after she arrived in Beantown, he found it more diplomatic to leave her behind during this difficult period. In fact, he chose to not even mention her name. He told me he could sense in their completely avoiding any mention of her that they were sure he would come to his senses about the "Irish Firebrand."

When he was away those weekends, I got to chaperone Siobhan. It was no easy task because Joe was right about the throw-herself-into-life thing. Siobhan was a party animal. The life of the party. The brothers loved her. She could toss back beers with the best of them. I was nowhere near her league in matters of alcohol and felt unfulfilled because of it. She'd arise on the Sunday mornings-after, from one-, maybe-two hours sleep on the couch in the game room, looking like she could go another day and night or two. I'd be in the bathroom on the second floor puking my guts out.

It was the third straight Saturday night Joe had been away. Siobhan and I were each nursing a bourbon from a bottle a brother from Kentucky had given me. He'd said my problem with booze was not a matter of quantity, but quality and he'd taken it upon himself to upgrade my intake. That night Siobhan bore a look I was not sure I'd ever seen before; in fact, it was more a demeanor, a head-to-toe kind of posture. She almost glowed. There was the hint of a flush to her cheeks, a softness to her eyes, a gentleness in her tone of a voice, a TLC quality in her body language. It was communicating something physical attaching to me.

"We can't continue meeting like this, Siobhan," I said, a bit whimsically, to redirect my mind away from wherever the hell it might be leading me. "Sneaking off to an absent brother's room to get away from all the noise downstairs and," I added with wry smile, "to enjoy cocktails for two in our own secluded rendez*vous*."

"Ah yes," she responded, in one of her practiced, playful tones, "Shakespeare reincarnated. Another of Michael's musical rhymes: cocktails for two, then rendez*vous*. Secluded no less. Clearly stolen from the Bard."

"Hey! Shakespeare again? Damn him!" Then adding with another smile, "That rhyme was mine."

"Another stolen rhyme?"

"Hey, you drag me up here every Saturday night when Joe's away . . . albeit not to stray. "

She just smiled and shook her head.

"This is the entertainment, baby," I said, with a toothy grin.

"OK, enough, before I have to call the poetry police."

"I'm just trying to keep my lips going, so they don't wrap themselves around the glass rim," I said, holding my drink aloft. "So I don't wake up with another Sunday hangover. I don't know how you do it, that great capacity you have for libation."

"Fret not, my liege," she replied. "It's an Irish thing. We're born with beer in our veins – and damn sight better beer than this American piss water. You see, our stomachs learn to ignore the presence of alcohol. On the other hand, this bourbon, here, it's more a reminder of my home down south."

"Is that what creates your glow? All that inflammatory alcohol in your bloodstream?"

'My glow?"

"Look at you. The lovely color of your cheeks, a softness in your eyes, the gentleness in your tone of a voice. There's even a TLC quality in your body language."

"Whoa there, Buster. The resident love poet in this animal house goes softly softer on me."

"Thanks," I said, taking another sip of my bourbon. "I think."

"I guess people only see the brassy side of me," she replied. "But I have a soft side, too. And, I like the softer side of a man."

Damn, I loved that lilt in her voice. And, I loved hearing her speak about me. I was seldom part of the conversation when she was chugging beers with the brothers and never the subject. But Siobhan and I were alone now, seated with our backs against the headboard on the single bed in a small room, two floors

above the core of the festivities. It was the room of one of our
senior brothers, one of the few single rooms in the house. Its
occupant had gone home to Rhode Island for the weekend. (He
did that often.) Siobhan had guided me to it. Clearly, it was a
place she and Joe had visited before. Now, it seemed a place she
viewed as an escape from the world, even if the world were not
that far away and in a partying mood. When she said earlier she
wanted to talk, she unburdened herself about Joe and her
exasperation with his family's attitude toward her. It was
obvious she needed someone to let this out with, someone other
than Joe. She'd said a number of times how much he thought of
me, which I could not figure out because I felt Joe and I didn't
even talk that much, if truth be told. But now, *she* was talking
about *me*. It was an odd turn in the conversation.

"I never thought of myself as soft," I offered lamely.

She turned toward me.

"Look at you. I'm embarrassing you," she said, smiling
tenderly. "Your face is getting redder."

It did that, my face.

"I wouldn't say I'm embarrassed," I countered, "I'm ..."

Her smile dissolved momentarily, then returned. It was a
gentle smile. She wasn't mocking me, certainly not intentionally
exposing a vulnerability I found uncomfortable to reveal.

"You shouldn't be distressed by your feminine side," she
said. "All those guys downstairs trying to grow hair on their
chests with alcohol and hootin' and hollerin'? They're like a
group of cats marking their territory, I don't find that the least
bit –"

"Feminine side?" I sputtered, the high-quality booze having
worked its way through my brain and out my lips. Now, she *was*
touching a nerve, whether she intended to or not. I'd grown up
in a working class neighborhood, where guys gained
respectability in street fights. All except me. I never fought.
And my friends never seemed to expect me to. I was the block
scholar. But that whole dynamic had me growing up doubting
my courage, sometimes even questioning my masculinity. And
now, somehow, she was reading this. And now, somehow, I was

realizing she was not focusing on something I had been shrinking from for years but was now connecting with this element she saw as something special in me.

"You really don't see this," she replied, "do you?"

"See what?"

She shifted her body weight and turned squarely in my direction. "This something, which sets you apart."

"Now I'm getting even more confused."

She stared into my eyes as if trying to burrow in behind them. "So then, mister poetry man, you've opened with some bad rhymes. Now how about something with feeling?

I stared at her, wide-eyed. "Really," I replied. "You really want that?"

She smiled warmly and nodded.

"OK then. I call this 'I Build Mountains in Midair,' or Why the Hell Am I Here and Not Where I Really Want To Be."

I paused for effect.

"Proceed," she replied.

> I build mountains in midair
> whose bases rest on clouds.
> I build my mountains over night
> on clouds of white, not grey or yellow.
>
> Midair mountains cannot crumble
> for they weigh less than a flea.
> Yet every so often they are heard to rumble
> and a tightness grows inside of me.
>
> But lengthy tremors are not allowed
> and work resumes then at the site,
> with changes only slight,
> still grey-less and un-yellow.
>
> For whoever heard of midair mountains
> surrounded by greys and yellows?

"Wow. That's really good, Michael," she replied. "I have no idea what you're talking about, but I know I like it."

"Welcome to free verse poetry."

"How come you don't share this work with others."

"And where would I do that? At Greasy Spoon downtown, for coins in my chip jar, after I flunk out of The Toot?"

"There's got to be an outlet for you," she replied. Then she shifted even closer to me and again stared deeply into my eyes. "This time something more . . . with feeling?"

I studied her look for a moment, then said, "A Picture, Perceived."

She nodded and I began:

> Form feints in the white light,
> Modulated whispers in ancient undocumented tongues
> Brush the coarse surface of the real.
> She feels. She is. She remains
> The path from the soft touch of the surreal
> . . . Siobhan.

Her eyes widened, her jaw went a bit slack, her look was utter astonishment. She got up and placed her drink down on the desk adjacent to the bed. She took my glass and did the same with it. She then shuffled back onto the bed and moved close to me, once again. Softly, she put her hand on the back of my neck and gently pulled my face close to hers. We kissed, then embraced, then slid down on the bed together.

What happened next was a defining moment in my life. Actually, what transpired during that all-to-brief period – less than an hour – was the experience that assured I might never find fulfillment with a woman, ever again. Others would be competing against an image, an ideal. I don't know if it was the alcohol, my almost total lack of experience, Siobhan's obvious abilities, or some combination of all of the above. Perhaps it was the fact that I was – had been – more in love with her than even Joe had been. Perhaps she'd have that effect on any man. But, if this was what connecting with a woman was about – connecting body and soul – well, then perhaps it was meant to be a once-in-a-lifetime experience.

*   *   *   *   *

When Joe returned on Sunday evening, he was looking particularly gloomy. I asked if his father had taken a turn for the worse, and he answered, "you might say that," almost flippantly. Reading my confusion at the tone of his reply, he said he had told his father he was going to ask Siobhan to marry him. "I didn't want him to die without knowing that, to not know who would be bearing his grandchildren," he went on. "I felt it would be dishonest to sneak her into the family after he died."

He paused for a moment, although I did not feel it was to await a response from me. "It was a mistake," he continued. "A big mistake. It upset him in a manner I had seen many times before, but it was clear my mother and my sister found it much more disconcerting this time, given his condition. My mother looked at me as if *I* were the cause of my father's terminal illness. My sister just smirked and shook her head."

Given what had transpired the night before, between Siobhan and me, it was clear Joe was having a rough couple of days. I wasn't too clear-headed myself. However, despite the haze that enveloped me for days after my encounter with Siobhan, I never doubted that she would marry Joe, irrespective of the cost to his family connection. It seemed to me preordained, no matter how much his family would try to prevent it. I knew then that she and I would never be more than that less-than-one-hour in that tiny room of the fraternity house, with the brothers banging on the door, shouting: "Mike!" then, "Siobhan, you in there?" But I don't think a bomber attack would have had an impact upon us. I had had that one-time encounter with the most beautiful woman in the world.

The smile she gave me every now and then, the sparkle that danced across her eyes, said we had shared something special, something I would not desecrate by divulging it to others, even though having her pelt would have elevated me into the

11

stratosphere with those hootin' and hollerin' assholes who were trying to grow hair on their chests. But I would be ever silent about it even if Joe did not hold me in such high regard.

Joe's father died shortly thereafter, but there was enough time for him to write Joe out of his will. He left everything to Joe's mother and sister and, while nothing in the will prohibited them from sharing some of the wealth with Joe, they held fast to his father's wishes, especially when it came to "the Irish girl."

"Fuck 'em," Joe said to me when he returned from the funeral. "I don't want any of his money, even if I have to work my way through the rest of this curriculum. I can make a damn good living with this level of education."

But Siobhan had plans, and they would take capital. She needled Joe to contest the will, insisting he hold out for at least the million dollars she felt the family would spend to stay out of court and out of the tabloids. She was right. The day after the family's attorney arranged a transfer to Joe's bank account, Joe and Siobhan eloped.

* * * * *

My remarkable academic recovery during my second semester at MIT had deluded me, momentarily, into thinking I could enjoy chemistry as my life's work, but by the middle of my third semester, I was sure thermodynamics and I were not bound for a lasting relationship. At the end of that semester, with my father's blessing, I transferred to NYU as a Liberal Arts major. I kept in touch with the Daltons and a couple of my fraternity brothers for a few more years, until my pledge class graduated, then pretty much put the MIT episode of my life behind me, save for a few chance encounters with brothers here and there . . . until Joe dropped me a note thirty-two years later. He'd found my home address through the fraternity mailing list. His letterhead included a phone number in Vermont, with a couple of zeroes at the end of it. He said he'd be on Long Island, near where I lived, for a few days on business, a few weeks hence, and would truly enjoy seeing me. "And, yes," his note ended, "I am thin on top and thick in the middle, so don't sweat your loss of youthful appearance. Siobhan sends her love."

My God.

I shook the cobwebs from my brain.

When I punched in the number he'd written, an operator answered, "Lake and Mountain Inn." She said Mr. Dalton was out of town, would I like his voice mail? I said yes and she connected me to a recorded voice I would have recognized had I spoken last to Joe the day before. I left a message, including my phone number and he called that evening. He said he was in Washington at a hotelier's convention but would love to see me when he was next in New York, those few weeks hence. "It's been too long, Mike. How could we let more than thirty years separate two good friends?"

Actually, I'd not given him much thought during most of that time, but I had to admit to myself seeing him again would be . . . interesting.

"My wife said she would have loved to accompany me down, but she's been having a hell of a time with the new addition to the hotel and she doesn't expect she'll have a handle on it by then." He stated that matter-of-factly, as if I would know what he was talking about, but, of course, it was Siobhan I was thinking about and wondering if the years had been good to her. "Anyway, she said to give you her love. You know she thinks the world of you, Mike."

"I . . . And I her."

Joe and I met at a restaurant not far from my home on the Island. He'd driven over from the posh Garden City Hotel in a rented Lexus. It was early spring, a damp, cold evening, and I found I couldn't shake the chill. Part of it was the sheer strangeness at seeing him again, the reinforcement of how little he meant to me, the instant recognition of how much his wife had altered the way I viewed life, the fatalistic attitude our encounter had created for me. We exchanged stories about families. They were childless; his problem. I had had a daughter with my ex-wife, all grown and pretty much out of my life, except for the obligatory holiday visits.

He was very impressed with the fact that I had had articles published in dozens of newspapers and magazines, and had written a couple of light-selling business books. I told him not to be too impressed, that my inability to earn any serious money had played a major role in my failed relationships. He related how just about everything in their lives revolved around the hotel, which Siobhan had turned into a real showplace. He said he had practiced engineering at a couple of firms for a while, but hated it, mostly hated working for someone. After a few years, he tried to match his interest in science and engineering with her love of the hotel, but mostly his operational concepts were either meddlesome or downright impractical. Now, he served pretty much as the hotel's ambassador to mostly meaningless industry functions.

"We'd like you to come and stay with us for a few days," he said. "Hell, stay as long as you like."

"I can't get away for too long," I fudged. "I'm working on a couple of projects and the deadlines are running up on me." I couldn't imagine what I would do for more than a few days at the hotel, while Joe and Siobhan went about their regular duties.

"Come for a long weekend," he pressed. "Stay at the hotel a couple of nights, then out at our house on the lake for a couple more. Wait until the weather warms. We'll go out in the boat." He paused for a moment, then, "she's done remarkable things with the hotel," he said, then paused again. We were into our second bottle of zinfandel and I could sense he was about to open up a bit, go down a road I might not find comfortable.

"It's not my real interest," he said, "the hotel. After a while, it all comes down to changing towels and bed linens and fielding phone calls from pissed-off patrons in the dead of night. But Siobhan, she has blossomed with the place. Wins awards. Has our hotel on the 'best' lists in all the best guidebooks and travel magazines. First name basis with the governor, both senators."

"What . . . ?" I took another swallow of zin. "What do you do with yourself all day?"

He looked at me and just shook his head. Then, he raised his glass of wine, held it up to the table lamp a moment and admired its rich, red color. "We have definitely upgraded the booze since Boston, haven't we?" he said finally.

"You mean it ain't Rock 'n Rye, a bottle o' Bud back?"

"Yeah," he said, nodding. His face lit into a full smile. "Dems was da daiz, weren't dey?"

"Yeah," I slurred. "The good ole days."

"See you in a few months?" He knew he had me now.

"Why not? It'll be good to see Siobhan again, now that I've seen your sorry ass," I answered brazenly.

He insisted upon picking up the check, despite my protests that he was on my turf. We shook hands outside the restaurant and headed for our cars. Even during the short ride home, I had enough time to ponder the irony of Siobhan, a successful hotelier – highly successful – while Joe, an MIT graduate, and I, an NYU grad, were still flopping around trying to find ourselves. It couldn't even be ascribed simply to the intense focus of her vision. I was doing exactly what I'd always felt would make me happy, even did a piece on baseball spring training for an airline magazine. Joe had started out in business doing what he'd always wanted, then, in essence, must have had to deal with whether that was, in fact, the case, or whether what he thought he had always wanted was just a matter of rebelling against an over-controlling father.

So what was I looking at here? Meeting Siobhan after more than thirty years, with my less-than-impressive resume. Perhaps I could gain some measure of dignity by presenting myself as doing a piece for some travel magazine or the travel section of one of the newspapers that bought my stuff from time to time, then drop back out of their lives.

*　*　*　*　*

Some unanticipated, fairly lucrative assignments kept me at home for several weeks longer than I'd anticipated and in the process provided me with some conversation pieces. So, it was not until late August, a hot and dry Wednesday, that I drove up to Vermont, leaving my home well before dawn so as to make it to the hotel in time for a late lunch, as Joe had suggested. The plan was for me to stay at the hotel Wednesday and Thursday nights, relocate to the Daltons' home on Lake Champlain for the weekend, then head back to Long Island on Monday.

From the moment I drove into the parking lot, then under the overhang beneath the façade, it was clear that the hotel was a work of art, obviously lavished with love. A bellhop had my bags out of the trunk, within seconds of my popping the lock, and deposited at the front desk a moment later, then disappeared before I could even consider tipping him.

The principal design feature of the main lobby was the highly varnished hardwoods throughout, huge structural timbers and beautifully carved accents strategically positioned along the walls and the ceiling. The counter at the front desk was a brilliant piece of Vermont marble, polished to a high sheen. The walls were papered in hunter green and hung in impressionistic-style paintings of woodland scenes. Beautiful sculptures in stone and metal were positioned about and wood carvings and pottery pieces stood on just about every horizontal surface. A fieldstone fireplace dominated a sitting room just off the main lobby. There was a small bar off to one side of the fireplace that advertised an afternoon tea service, via an elegantly lettered sign resting on a brass easel.

The desk clerk said that Mrs. Dalton had left word for me to get checked in, after which I was to notify the front desk and she would meet me in the lobby for lunch in the dining room. A bellhop led me to a room, beautifully furnished in large mahogany pieces, a giant four-poster bed, an antique chifforobe and two beautifully carved end tables, one on either side of the bed. A fireplace with a supply of perfectly aligned wood chunks in a wrought-iron cradle conjured up images of dancing flames on a cold winter's night. By contrast, the bathroom was a thoroughly modern affair, including a whirlpool that would have accommodated two comfortably. If I were not so anxious to see Siobhan, I would have had difficulty leaving the room, but instead, I stowed my gear then headed back to the desk, whereupon the clerk rang Siobhan's office. I took the seat, suggested by the desk clerk, in the oversized chair next to the fireplace, now merely hinting at its winter coziness in the heat of the mid-summer afternoon.

Siobhan glided into the room less than ten minutes later. She was as striking as ever, her beauty little tempered by the three decades that had separated us, save for the predictable crows' feet around those devastating green eyes and the closer-cropped, carefully coiffed taming of that great mane of red hair. She had put on a bit of weight, but I could tell by the way she still moved with such an undeniable grace and rhythm that it had been distributed in all the right places.

"Michael," she said, in that voice that passed through me like a velvet X-ray, "where have you been hiding?"

"Obviously, in all the wrong places," I said, taking the hand she offered, then boldly kissing her cheek.

She smiled broadly. "Joe is in town, running late at a meeting of his engineers group," she said. "He still likes to keep his hand in, but he said not to wait lunch for him."

She ushered me across the lobby to the dining room, built onto that part of the hotel furthest from the front entrance, atop a grassy area overlooking a small duck pond. A series of floor-to-ceiling glass panels let in the bright summer light, filtered through gauzy, off-white curtains. Glass doors opened onto a wide patio, which would make for wonderful outdoor affairs, weather permitting.

"You and Joe have made a real success of your life together," I remarked as the hostess showed us to our table. "A real tribute to your marriage."

She didn't answer immediately, then, "Joseph and I haven't been doing so well, in recent years," she said before I'd even settled into my seat. "I know he didn't tell you that on his trip to New York, or in subsequent telephone conversations, because he was afraid you'd decide not to come."

I had no idea how to respond. Fortunately, the waitress was standing alongside with the menus, large leather-bound affairs more suited to an elegant dinner than a simple lunch.

"I'm sure he'll tell you about it when he gets here," she continued after the waitress had left and Siobhan had placed her menu alongside her table setting. "Try the seafood bisque and the cold lobster salad. They're exquisite."

I still hadn't said a word since we'd entered the dining room, it occurring to me that I was one-on-one with the woman who had created the most memorable moment of my life – in a singular situation with her for the first time since that moment – and she was telling me that she and her husband – ostensibly a good friend of mine – were having marital problems.

"I've had more than my share of failed relationships," was all I could muster, finally, as if that put their failing marriage into context, or perhaps to show that even if they did split up, their marriage would have lasted considerably longer than any of my relationships.

"I'm so sorry to hear that, Michael," she said, with that sincere concern in her voice and that wonderful softness in her eyes, as if now, suddenly, my problems needed more attention than hers.

"Oh, it was for the better for both of us," I replied, "and besides, it was some time ago."

Sadness darkened the softness in her eyes. "I'm sorry," she repeated. "You deserved better, Michael."

No, I thought, no, I did not deserve better. I'd fucked up in choosing a woman for my wife whom I should have known would never be right for me. What was it with her and her husband and their unshakably positive opinions of me, based on no good evidence?

"Maybe so," I said finally. "Maybe I did deserve better, but I really didn't do much to make that happen." I shook my head, gazed at her a moment, even more amazed at how good the years had been to her. Even the added roundness to her face had a softening effect, seemed to broaden the natural blush to her cheeks. "I mean look at you," I said, then added quickly, "look at all you've accomplished."

"Yes," she answered, her tone softening further, "all I ever wanted in life."

We were both silent a while, then, "Why am I here, Siobhan?" I asked.

She dropped her gaze to her fidgeting fingers, uncharacteristically avoiding eye contact, then she raised her eyes again and said, "Joe seems to think it can help. That you will be good for us."

The comment was one more absurdity in what I had always considered a strange relationship; for me, in neither case, a real friendship. It might have set me off on some potentially embarrassing diatribe to that effect if the waitress had not arrived to take our order. I took the soup and lobster salad; Siobhan some standing special order of greenery and mineral water.

"And you, Siobhan," I asked when the waitress had retreated, "what do you think?"

I guess there must have been a lingering edge to my voice. Her frown told me she was less convinced than Joe that I could help, or perhaps she didn't like the question. "I don't know," she said, feebly. "I'm sure it can't hurt." The comment described the less-than-dramatic effect I had had on so many things in my life.

I stared at her a while. I wanted to ask if that tangle of limbs that had, for one brief and, for me, shining moment, defined our relationship had also, with some sense of irony, made me uniquely qualified to help her and her husband rebuild their marriage. But, of course, I did not.

Fortunately, lunch provided the easy exit from the uncomfortable conversation. It was every bit as exquisite as Siobhan had promised, but that did not surprise me. And things lightened up somewhat when she said, "Oh hell, Michael, enjoy your stay here. This is a great spot, especially this time of year. Let's hoist a few brews like in days gone by and forget the fiddle-dee-dah life serves up." She smiled broadly, an infection that spread to my face. "Now, tell me about some of the good things you've done."

There were some, of course, and it felt good to share them with her. It all managed to brighten the conversation a bit further. We parted with warm smiles and an appointment to gather as the trio of old for some fun times the following evening.

*   *   *   *   *

When Joe caught up with me that afternoon, he said nothing about his problematic marriage, nothing. I assumed Siobhan had advised him that she had taken care of that unpleasantness. While I was a bit on edge about the possibility of the subject eventually coming up the times Joe and I would be alone together, the concern dissipated as I spent some time with myself, merely enjoying the surroundings: bookended by a martini on the patio before dinner and bourbon neat out there before bed.

The next morning, after breakfast, I did some laps in the hotel's indoor swimming pool. After lunch, the hotel masseur kneaded the knots I'd been building up at the base of my neck for years. That afternoon, on an impulse, I bought a book on northeastern birds in the hotel gift shop, then took a walk in the woods behind the hotel and even identified a rose-breasted grosbeak and a red-bellied woodpecker.

There was a renewed gaiety when the three of us got together, that evening. It *was* great hoisting a few brews, as she had put it, at the bar in the pub in the basement of the hotel, which even reminded me of the game room in the basement of the fraternity house. I accused Joe of having had it designed that way. He blamed Siobhan and she flashed me that gleam.

We spent a couple of hours the next afternoon batting little white balls around on the pitch-and-putt course in back of the hotel and getting sillier and sillier with each beer we fished out of a cooler we dragged around the course with us. I sensed they had not done much of any of this lately, perhaps not in years, at least not unless it fulfilled some obligation to their guests. So, perhaps my presence *was* having a therapeutic effect on their marriage. Perhaps it was a catalyst for a renewed look at the more pleasant aspects of their life together. Perhaps, that's what I was: a catalyst in other people's lives. Never a principal player, never even a part of the solution, just someone who disappeared once the parties had coalesced into their special chemistry. When Siobhan and Joe went to tend to a few duties before we would be relocating to their place, things were beginning to focus for me: this sense that I had been simply an observer, someone lurking about the edges of life. Hell, it was what a writer did; well, a writer like me anyway. Perhaps other people sensed that what reflected back off me would somehow make things clearer for them, and they fed off that, used it.

As I finished repacking, Joe called and said to meet them out front with my car and we'd head out. I said, I hadn't checked out yet, but he replied it had been taken care of. There was no point even offering a feigned protest. I hoisted my bags and headed for the parking lot, tossed them into the trunk of my car, then followed their car out to their home on Lake Champlain.

The house had been the summer place of a lawyer Joe knew, who sold it to the Daltons when his marriage unraveled. Siobhan had been the instigator on the deal, having fallen in love with the location, while her mind raced through all the designs of interiors and exteriors she would implement to create her dream home. They'd left the original house in place, but gutted it completely and turned the space into three large, open rooms: a dining room that stepped down into a living room, forming the perfect combination for entertaining groups from a single couple to a small crowd; a Florida room, set off by a wall, with only a small archway, its major feature an expansive entertainment center with all the bells and whistles; and the largest kitchen I'd ever seen, with restaurant-class appliances. Four bedrooms were added along the west side of the original structure, each with plenty of space and its own bathroom. All the bedroom windows opened onto the lake, and, with their westward facing, took full advantage of the sunsets. A deck ran around all sides of the house, except for the front.

"How about I stir up a pitcher of martinis?" Siobhan suggested, after showing me about the house. We had the drinks on the deck with a selection of cheeses and fruits. I slept, that night, like someone taken off life support.

* * * * *

The following morning I awoke to the smell of frying garlic, splashed some water on my face, pulled on a pair of cotton slacks and a polo shirt, slipped into a pair of Docksiders and went out as she was sliding a delicious smelling omelet onto a serving dish. I poured myself a cup of coffee and joined the Daltons for breakfast. They said they needed to tend to some scutwork at the hotel but assured me I had the run of the house. "Relax. Take a dip in the lake," Joe suggested. "Just hang out. Whatever."

After my hosts departed, I sat in an Adirondack chair on the deck behind the Daltons' house that Saturday in August, mid-morning, taking inventory of my life. I found there had been other Joes, other Siobhans, people I had met along my many seemingly aimless routes through life, somehow sensing this strange power I had to create, or reflect back, the answers they were seeking, the solutions they required. Even that fateful episode with Siobhan, that unquestionably, uncommonly participatory less-than-one-hour with Siobhan, seemed, in retrospect, merely to have provided her the final push into Joe's arms. My big moment had only been the catalyst for his bigger moment and my unwillingness to talk about it, even with my co-participant, had forever consigned it to the fate of a non-event. I mean did she even remember it? Should I ask? There was an unquestionable element of confrontation should I decide, after all these years, to nudge this long dormant issue back out into the light of day and confrontation was not something I did. I just wrote about when other people did it. And that was that. You did not opt for such a sea change this late in the voyage. At least, I didn't.

I sat, my mind suddenly blank. It was a comfort. No analyses. No strategies. No ulterior motives. No objectives. No. . . thoughts. Except for the sensory experience that was the landscape before me. The beautiful panorama before me.

It had been an abnormally dry summer in the northeast, with the preceding four weeks devoid of any rain, save for a barely measurable trace here and there. The drought had dropped the level of the big lake to where you could see stretches of the rocky shale bottom, in areas normally submerged under several feet of water. The thin, vertical sheets of shale looked like records in an old Wurlitzer, their sharp edges looking quite menacing, however. They said look, but don't venture forth. In the distance, small islands sat like clumps of blue-gray clay in the white mist that ran to the edges of the horizon. An overturned canoe languished in a patch of beige grass, the boat's fiberglass underside growing a crystalline white crust in the heat of the sun. Just beyond the deck, between two Adirondack chairs that gazed out toward the lake, a cluster of black-eyed Susans waved in the intermittent breeze, the petals darkened to a burnt orange by the crackled air. I considered a swim but did not want to negotiate the mean-looking shale; considered a spin in the kayak, dismissed it. Sat, motionless.

Ask her.

The thought held for a moment, then faded like a muffled drum.

Suddenly, my eye caught a tiny glint of light, immediately bleeding into a thread of liquid silver, swinging through the shadow cast by the eave directly above me. The hair-thin pendulum of light, then disappeared in the sunlight just beyond the shadow. The vestige spark of a memory unable to hold on. Its absence drew my eye back to the lakescape before me and the Zen-like quality of an emptied mind.

Ask her.

A moment later, the liquid thread captured my interest once again. This time, I was determined not to let it hide in the sunlight. I stayed with it, followed its length to the tiny, gray-brown ball at its terminus. A spider was knitting a web across the tall heads of some withered daisies in a wooden flower box, which ran the length of the deck. He seemed pressed to finish this project within some predetermined timetable and he went determinedly about it, swinging back and forth, attaching threads as he went. When the spider had decided he'd completed his work, he dropped a line straight down, landed upon my sandal, stayed a moment to get his bearings, then raced away along the deck and disappeared, leaving me the momentary spectator of his one-act play now connected only by the silken thread of his descent. I shook my foot back and forth until the thread broke free.

With the rising heat of the summer day, the thought of the morning shower I had been putting off had become more and more irresistible. Just outside the door to the hallway that ran between the house's master bedroom and the guestroom where I was staying stood an outdoor shower, an L-shaped barrier combining with the exterior of the house to provide privacy. It was a small luxury Siobhan had decided the house needed, after luxuriating in one at a resort hotel in the Caribbean. When she'd showed me it during my intro tour about the house, she'd gone on about the unexpected pleasures of taking a shower in the outside air. She said she took her morning shower in it as long as the warm weather permitted, sometimes pushing it right up to the days when overnight freezes left a coating of hoarfrost on the deck. They had blown the water pipe three times during hard night frosts, Joe told me.

I pushed myself out of the chair and padded off to my room to slip out of my clothes.

*   *   *   *   *

After dinner that night, Joe and I sat on the back deck with a pitcher of drinks, while Siobhan puttered around with household chores. He seemed introspective, said little, grew more taciturn with his second martini. Slurring his words during the third drink, he shared the news that he had gotten a call that day from his sister, whom he said he hadn't heard from in years. She'd said their mother was gravely ill. Doctors felt she had no more than a few days to live.

"My sister said, despite my self-imposed exile from the family all these years, my mother wanted to see me." His tone

was lugubrious. "My sister has her way with the facts," he
added, with as much irony as his drunken, hesitant speech
would allow. "Perhaps it would ease my mother's final moments
if I told her Siobhan and I were splitting up. It would close the
circle I'd opened when my father died."

He lowered his gaze to the thin-stemmed martini glass in his
right hand, raised the glass and took a sip. I studied him a
moment, trying to ascertain if he were finally opening up about
his marriage or merely toying with some allusion to his fucked-
up family situation, but he let go of the subject and betrayed
nothing more of his feelings.

"I need to drive on over to Boston tomorrow," he said,
"Early, so I'll excuse myself. I'll be spending a night or more
there, in a hotel of course, so I'll probably not see you again
before you leave, Mike. I'm sorry."

"No need, at all, to apologize," I said. "I understand
completely."

He rose from his chair. "You must come see us again,
sometime," were his parting words.

"I will . . . see," I answered, but his back was to me and he
was already retreating down the hall to the master bedroom,
sliding a hand against the wall to steady himself.

Siobhan and I finished our drinks, making only small talk. It
was clear that if she wanted to unburden herself further on this
whole family thing and the more critical issue of her marriage's
future, tonight was not the night she would do that. I helped her
with some left over cleaning up, then went to bed.

*   *   *   *   *

Sunday, they were both gone before I arose. I needed to get
away, so I spent the day visiting art galleries and antique shops,
had lunch at a sandwich shop in a tiny town, then circled back
toward the Dalton house and had dinner at an outdoor café in
Burlington.

When I got back to the house it was empty, so I took up my
familiar position in the Adirondack chair on the back deck, now

in the light of early evening, watching the sky deepen to purple and the clouds capture what light was left in undersides of salmon. I was trying to get myself back into that blank mindset I'd begun to find so strangely liberating when I heard the slap of the screen door against the doorjamb at the front of the house. Immediately thereafter, I could hear sounds coming from the kitchen and was expecting her momentarily on the back deck, with a hello and perhaps one of the martinis we had become so fond of during my visit. Instead, the kitchen sounds ended abruptly and I was returned to the insect buzz of the thickening night. I considered getting up to go find her, but I knew she knew that I was in the house or about the grounds and that she would find me when she was ready.

The darkness had brought an orange glow to the porch lamps, which were mounted atop poles at intervals along the deck rail, with sensors activated by the falling light. Far out in the lake, a full moon began to peek above the islands. A screech owl made its presence known from within a dense stand of hemlocks. The natural sounds of the night were interrupted by the rush of water from the head of the outdoor shower and the splatter of the spray hitting the deck floor. Within a few moments, the timbre of the shower spray altered as the course of the water was redirected by her body. The cool flow of that cascade, the cleansing foam of the soap dissolving the sticky, oily residues of a hot August day must have felt luscious in the midst of the hot, windless night. My recently vacant mind was now filled with images of the water running over the marvelous contours of her body, pushing the clusters of soap bubbles before it, adding a fresh liquid sheen to her flesh. I was consumed by the changing tone of the water force, the sounds of the spray, the soft clap of it against her body, the occasional plop as she swept water down her breasts and over her abdomen. And then the water music was gone, with that finality of a closed spigot.

A few minutes later, I could hear the falls of her wet feet as she stepped around the wooden barrier, the slap growing louder . . . as she approached the corner of the deck where I sat, now a faint shadow in the grayness, all but hidden in the muted lamplight. She was walking in a direct line toward the back door to the kitchen, holding a bath towel loosely around her, unaware of my presence. Then, "Oh!" she said, the towel falling away, as she started. "Michael. I didn't see you there." She fumbled to retrieve the towel and pull it back around her, holding the edges together with her left hand behind her back.

"I'm sorry," I answered. "I didn't mean to startle you, but I felt whether I said something or not, either way I might frighten you. I'm sorry."

"Oh, it's all right," she said. "It's all right. I should have come to find you when I got home. It's just that it's so hot and I was dying to jump into the shower."

"Yes," I replied, "the sound of the water was a very inviting one."

The corners of her mouth curled into the hint of that sly smile, which just sent shivers up my spine. It was downright coquettish. "You should do it," she said. "It will un-rankle you."

I didn't know I sounded . . . rankled, but . . . perhaps I did. "I think I will," I said.

"Take your time," she answered. "I'll fix us a pitcher of martinis."

"Wonderful."

I made my way to my bedroom, undressed in the darkness and wrapped a large bath towel about me, then headed down the hall past the master bedroom, out the door at the end of the corridor, then around the barrier and into the shower. I draped the towel over the top of the barrier, turned on the water, adjusted it to a refreshing temperature and stepped into its soothing rush. There were still streaks of soapsuds along the walls and bubbles still clinging to the bar of soap in the dish. I picked up the soap, almost reverentially, applied it directly to my body and began working up a lather, stuck on the thought that she had done the same, mere minutes before.

I let the cool torrents run over me, wash the lather over the length of my body. As she had suggested, it took my "rankles" with it. It was such a soothing process; I felt I could stand there forever, but finally turned off the water. I reached for the towel, pulled it down from the barrier and rubbed myself vigorously, then ran my fingers back through my hair to get it out of my eyes and into some semblance of order.

A breeze rustled the trees and fingered through the slats in the shower barrier, brushing over the remaining moisture on my skin and making me feel about as cool and refreshed as I had ever felt in my life. I draped the towel back over the barrier and just stood there breathing in the naturally scented air and letting the soft wind continue to do its thing with my body. It was having the effect of nullifying any tensions that remained, especially from this whole confusing encounter with the Daltons and the numbing effects of trying to understand my role in this strange process. I closed my eyes and tried, as I had done earlier, to empty my mind and conjoin with the natural environment. It was a glorious feeling.

And then I felt it. The intrusion of her presence.

"Why is it all so wrong, Michael?" she said. She was standing there, beyond the opening to the shower, naked, the glow of the porch lamps scribing the thinnest rim-light around her form. "All the pieces are in place. So why is it so very wrong?"

I'm sure my eyes had widened and my jaw had gone slack, but she was totally nonplused by her nakedness and mine. "I don't know, Siobhan," I said. "I don't know." I wanted to say, why would I know? In my life, seldom have even a few of the pieces been in place and yet, what she was telling me, in so many words, was that my life had not turned out all that different from hers.

She was staring at the floor, now, shaking her head barely perceptibly. I was riveted to the spot. If anyone had described this improbable scenario in advance, an inability to move from the spot, close the distance between us, embrace the pure beauty of the naked woman before me, it would not have been the outcome I'd have predicted. Then, as if only at that moment realizing she was naked, she picked up the towel from where it lay on the deck at her feet, draped it across the front of her body

and sat down on the deck bench opposite. She was sobbing
softly.

I took my towel from over the shower barrier, wrapped it
tightly about my lower half and tucked the edge into the waist to
keep it closed. Then I went and sat alongside her, leaving
enough space for propriety's sake. She sobbed a short while
longer, then fought it to a stop. But she said nothing, just
continued to stare down at the deck between her feet. I could
think of nothing appropriate to break the silence.

Finally, "Michael," she said, "why did you not . . ." The words
trailed off.

"What?" I muttered.

She raised her head and looked me full in the face. "Why did
you not come to me? Then. In Boston."

"Come to you?" I questioned.

"Yes, after . . .

My brow furrowed, my mouth fell open. "I . . . You . . . You
were Joe's . . . sweetheart."

She shook her head slightly, held her gaze to mine. "No," she
said. "Certainly not after that night."

"But?" There were just no more words to add.

"I never was his. Not to this day. I left Virginia because
there was nothing for me there and Joe was a fun ticket out. We
made no promises to each other, beyond enjoying a mutual
friendship. Even when we had sex, it was casual, light-hearted,
two young people experimenting with each other's bodies. I
thought that's all it would ever be, with anyone. Until that night
with you."

"W-we were drunk, Siobhan, plastered. I thought we had
simply fallen under the spell of the alcohol, made a big mistake,
at the expense of my friend and your lover."

Sadness began to infuse her eyes. "Then, did you not feel
it?" she asked.

I didn't know how to reply, having carried that moment
around in my heart for all those years. "That was such a long
time ago, Siobhan," was my sorry answer.

The sadness in her eyes deepened. "I had never felt such a connection before," she replied. "Never since." She shook her head. "I had only prayed that you had felt the same, Michael. Perhaps it was merely my pathetic need to have had you feel as I did. My belief that I could not have experienced such a connection if you had not as well."

I was dumbfounded. She stared at me a moment longer, then her body stiffened as she prepared to rise. I placed a hand on her shoulder to stop her and I could feel the tenseness go out of her. In that instant, in the sultry heat of that August night, with the thin layer of perspiration beginning to coat the contours of her body and the sweet smell of her joining with the aromas of the land and the lake, there and then, I wanted her more than I'd ever wanted anything before . . . or since. In that instant, as my eyes met hers, all that we were feeling for each other passed, wordlessly, between us . . . and then was gone.

She rose from the bench, an instant after I envisioned the great sense of loss, the irretrievable loss of well-being that would accompany her doing that. She tightened the towel about her and said, "I'll get the martinis."

"Great," I replied. I knew we both realized that, unlike the uninhibiting effect of all that alcohol that long ago night in Boston, this round of drinks would bring down the curtain on the lives that never were. I watched the lovely rhythm of her movement disappear behind the swinging screen door into the kitchen. The night that lay before me now was just a collage of formless elements, a series of dull and meaningless grays.

TUMBLEWEED

🎵 It never rains. It never snows.
That God-damned wind
just blows and blows. 🎵

From late winter to the onset of summer, the wind blows out of the west across the eastern New Mexico plateau with such force it lifts the crimson dirt of the bone-dry land into great red clouds, disheveled thunderstorms laden with grit instead of water, chasing vanquished armies of rolling tumbleweed, racing in all directions to escape the onslaught. Windows in the houses are locked down tight, even sealed with masking tape, but to little effect, as tiny red dunes form on windowsills in a mockery of any wet rags, which would turn them to crimson-colored mud. The red dust whistles beneath garage doors, collects on engine blocks in automobiles, creeps beneath the coverings of outdoor grills, dusts the green leaves of any garden plants, which survive the wind's fury.

My first reaction, of course, was visceral. She was the incarnation of a '60s chick, in a place where you'd least expect to find her: the Eastern New Mexico/West Texas plateau. Here, the only skyscrapers were oil rigs and grain silos; the music was not Big Brother and the Holding Company. Nonetheless, *she* was a reminder of the braless chicks back in Greenwich Village, who were just into their more aggressive, feminist-expression stages when I'd been forced to leave to go fight a war on the Indochina Peninsula, where, honestly, I really didn't have any argument with anyone and certainly not enough of a reason to kill any of them, let alone . . . well, them me. I was not much of a warrior.

She was in Janis Joplin mode, loose-fitting tank top, multiple beaded necklaces draped above her breastbone, bangles hanging from her ears and both her wrists; big, round eyeglasses. I was wondering if the getup were some kind of movie promotion and asked her. But she just smirked, then flashed me a sly, crooked smile. "It's a western movie, cowboy" she said, "not a Beatles flick." She tore off my ticket and pointed me toward the entrance to the seating area of the theatre. Well, I mused as I took my seat, she knows who The Beatles are.

The movie theatre had managed a fifteen-year-old copy of the western classic "Shane," with Alan Ladd, and honestly, it was either that or one more after-dinner night of drinking at the Officer's Club with a group of regular Air Force lifers, who had little in common with me and my pacifist politics. She, on the other hand, was something you could turn on to just thinking about her sly, crooked smile and that curvy, young-woman body, begging to be caressed in bed back at the bachelor officers' quarters, where there was nothing to do, each night, except hope sleep came early enough at the BOQ to prepare you for the predawn launches of F-100 fighters every morning . . . and hope my participation in the escalating war in southeast Asia would somehow hold off long enough, while I counted the days until I was FIGMO, as in "Fuck-it I Got My Orders," and left all this behind.

While it could be said, the initial attraction was just visceral, perhaps it was simply some vestige of muscle memory, a connection that I was yearning to reconstitute with any woman who was not in uniform or wearing a cowgirl hat. Nonetheless, from that moment forward, things just took their own course. Or maybe it *was* love at first sight. At least for me anyway. However, those *are* years of raging hormones and it turned out she really was something in bed. But I'm getting way ahead of myself.

I'd met her in 1968, the last year of my four-year tour in the Air Force. I was convinced the military had sent me to Cannon Air Force Base, just outside of Clovis, New Mexico, in the dry, warmer clime of the southwestern United States, that final year, as a lame attempt to get me to reenlist, after three years in the snow and ice fields of Minot, North Dakota. They'd tried to sweeten the pie further by promoting me to captain and assigning me chief of quality control on a fighter base, where we trained pilots in combat tactics to provide close air support for the ground troops fighting in South Vietnam. A career as an aircraft maintenance officer instead of the acclaim I'd receive as a writer once I reclaimed some literary territory back in New York City? I don't think so.

The transition to military service, three years earlier, from a senior year at New York University, in lower Manhattan, where I was an editor of the college newspaper, to US Air Force Officer Training School, in San Antonio, Texas, was a difficult contrast for me to process. I'd gone from big man on campus to small man in a military training program where some former high school fuck-up with a strange way of pronouncing words – aka drill sergeant – was shouting at me and all the other officer trainees, for our lack of competence in marching, failing white-glove inspections of our barracks rooms, or being unable to shower and shave in less than seven minutes, all of us having scabbed-up faces as badges of our incompetence.

So, as this final chapter, I had been exiled to the red-dust, tumbleweed-dancing plateau here in West Texas/Eastern New Mexico. With just a year left in my commission, I found I was longing, more intensely than ever, for a return to the incredibly creative cultural scene that was Greenwich Village of the 1960s, hopefully not too-advanced from where I'd left it as to be unrecognizable, a place where I could ditch buzzed-crew cut blind obedience and once again reclaim long-haired free expression. I needed avant-garde foreign films at the cinema, not Clint Eastwood, made-in-Italy westerns, in a dingy, cow-town movie house. I needed progressive bebop at downtown New York jazz joints, folk music and beat poets at the coffee houses along Bleecker Street just south of the fountain in Washington Square Park and the hope that I'd made it back to "The Village" before the girls had started wearing bras again.

Alternatively, in my current life, all I had was a steady diet of loud country and western bands at the CattleLac Bar, with the nightly fight outside in the parking lot between local cowboys and drunken airmen. For my own drink-driven desperation, there was The PoleKitten Lounge to watch nubile young cowgirls, in ten-gallon hats and little else, enticing drunken patrons to slip folding money into their G-strings. That the San Francisco topless bar model had made it as far as the scrublands of eastern New Mexico was a surprise even if it was late in the '60s. Nonetheless, it was only after too-many rounds at the O Club that any of us officers with reputations to uphold would slink off together and slide into the place. But no amount of paper money slipped into G-strings was likely to be the opening salvo for a physical relationship, no matter how many rum-and-cokes made that prospect seem more and more likely.

Imagine my surprise then when the local theatre listed "In the Heat of the Night," as its feature one week, the racially charged movie whose plot forces Rod Steiger's white southern lawman to work with Sidney Poitier's visiting black northern detective to solve a murder in a southern town. The movie, ultimately the Academy Award Winner, did not disappoint, but the real feature attraction for me the night I went to see it was, once again, the girl who took my ticket. Again the Janis Joplin garb, again my comment about a movie promotion, this time just to get her attention. Again her quippy rejoinder: "It's about racism in the deep south," she said. "Say, haven't I seen you someplace before?" Sexy, crooked smile.

"Yes," I responded, "you saw me here."

She just looked me over, handed back my ticket stub and moved on to the next patron.

My attraction to her was getting too difficult to ignore, but I had to move any future meeting to somewhere other than thirty seconds at the movie theatre. So, one evening, a week later, I drew on three years of ingrained military combat-readiness, bought a ticket for "Coogan's Bluff," Clint Eastwood's latest oater, and waited for the movie to be well underway before entering the theatre and what I would hope, at that point, would be an empty lobby. So far so good. I handed her my ticket. She ripped off the body of it and handed me back the stub. This time, her smile seemed to convey a modicum of warmth. I smiled back at her and asked if I could take her to dinner at the Officers' Club some evening, forcing the encounter so quickly there would be time to beat a hasty retreat should her response warrant it. Although I knew I would feel terribly exposed in this public setting, I'd also done my best to make sure only she and me would witness her rejection. I couldn't believe I was still so insecure as to worry about how this would be perceived by the one movie-goer who might come back to the lobby to use the restroom.

The question caught her completely off guard. "Officer's Club?" she replied, her eyebrows scrunching together. "Dinner?"

"Sure," I countered, "Why the questioning look?"

"You an officer?" she asked, adopting her sexy, almost-child-like, crooked smile.

"Captain . . . at Cannon."

"Captain?" she said, her eyes now studying my face with intensity. "You don't look old enough."

"They're promoting us younger, with so many experienced officers bailing out of reenlisting on account of Vietnam."

She studied me a while longer, eyebrows un-scrunching, but crooked smile returning, then, "sure," she said, "why not."

Although the answer I was looking for came quickly, it wasn't exactly a ringing endorsement. I reasoned, perhaps dating cowboys with steer shit on their boots and OD'd on too many Coors; or teenaged enlisted men with negative IQs may have begun to set her, however reluctantly, on a course into the lower echelon of life in this dusty, lifeless territory. So, I was hoping that may have pushed her to maybe, just maybe, think about trying something higher up the food chain.

Clearly, I *had* been over-thinking all this.

Unaware of all my silent analyses, her smile wrinkled a bit further. "Sure," she repeated. "I can do that."

"Mike Rhodes," I said, extending my hand.

"Aldina Connor," she said, taking my hand in a soft, tentative grasp.

"How's Friday evening?" I asked, not wasting any time to press my newly achieved advantage.

"We're busy here Friday and Saturday nights," she said.

"Oh yes, of course."

Again, the eyebrows scrunching. She studied me a moment again, then, "I'll get someone to cover for me," she replied.

"Great," I said, "if you can do that."

"O . . . K," she replied, and continued to study me, as if to discern something about me that wasn't on the surface. It was making me less sure that I had fully accomplished my objective this evening. "Can I call you?" I asked. "To confirm."

Now she turned her head and looked at me with a bit of a sideways glance. I read it, telegraphing that she was wondering why I was doubting what she had just agreed to.

"To confirm that you got someone to cover."

"Sure," she said, her look easing a touch. "Why not."

I fished a pen out of my shirt pocket and handed it to her along with the ticket stub. She wrote a phone number on the stub and handed it back to me.

"I'll call you mid-week to work out a time and find out where to pick you up," I said.

"I'm off Wednesdays," she said. "I live with my aunt and uncle. My aunt is home most of the day. If I'm not there, she'll take a message."

"Of course," I replied. "Call you then." I stood there a moment, not quite sure what to do next.

"Enjoy the movie," she said, condemning me to the ostensible reason for my coming there that evening.

During the remaining hour-and-a-half of "Coogan's Bluff," thoughts of Aldina twinkled across the violent scenes like a fairy godmother with a magic wand.

As I headed home that chilly night in early spring, the quiet was deafening, the hours of calm, before the winds would blow again at dawn.

* * * * *

My date with Aldina at the Officers' Club was awkward. She seemed intimidated by the surroundings: junior officers and their wives getting louder with each drink; senior staff officers, members of an older generation, relating war stories that had little relevance even to me, let alone to her. There were a half-dozen unaccompanied women, wives of pilots and support officers who were in Vietnam. The scene was awkward for me, as well, since Aldina was too young, at nineteen, to be served any alcohol, so we both had to settle for soft drinks with dinner. I tried to turn the conversation away from what was going on at the bar.

"Tell me something about yourself," I said. "I know it's a lame request, but how else do I start to get to know you?"

She smiled for the first time since we'd sat down. "You wanna know why I've chosen a career as a ticket-taker at a cow-town movie theatre, right?"

"There," I replied, "we've broken the ice. From ticket-taker to up on the silver screen in just a year or two." I gave her my toothiest smile.

"As a matter of fact, I *am* taking acting classes at Enemy U."

"Enemy U?"

37

"Eastern New Mexico University, just south of here in Portales."

"Movie star, hah. I would have guessed lead singer in a rock 'n' roll band."

"And why's that?"

"The Janis Joplin getup?"

"Oh, and I'm not allowed to like the blues, too?"

"Double career. Impressive."

"Nonetheless, you are asking yourself, college student? Why is she taking tickets at the movie house night after night?"

"Hey! I'm a journalist. I'll ask the questions here."

"Actually, I thought we'd moved beyond that. Nonetheless, to answer *your* question, I also work in the office, even have a say in what films they choose. But I also have to take tickets each evening to earn my pay."

And so it went for almost an hour. I felt we were making some headway in getting to know each other, although there were awkward moments when neither one of us could think of anything to say.

As our dinner was winding to a close, her attention was turned again back toward the bar. A guy was becoming louder with each new round of drinks, several times contradicting his wife sarcastically and clearly making her uncomfortable with his demeaning comments. Aldina kept studying the scene and alternately looking away, projecting a growing sense of discomfort each time.

"That major's an asshole," I said, finally. "Nobody likes him. He gets drunk at the O Club bar almost every night. Sometimes he's too hungover to fly on days he is assigned to, so he writes up nonexistent malfunctions with the airplanes. The mechanics then must go looking for problems they know don't exist."

"He beats up on his wife," she said, her look hardening, as if my explanation didn't get to the core of the problem.

"Maybe you're right," I answered. "I only ever see him when he's busting chops on the flight line and occasionally, when he's loud here at the bar."

Fortunately, the waitress arrived with our desserts. As we were finishing up, the drunker officers at the bar began singing a song that one of our former guitar-playing colleagues had composed the night before he returned to civilian life. They were just getting started singing the chorus over and over:

"It never rains,
it never snows
that God-damned wind
just blows and blows."

I knew next would come the increasingly risqué limerick stanzas and God-damned would become "fuckin'."
"That's it," I said. "The time when those of us who are not part of that group, know it's time to go."
It also forced the question I'd been mentally struggling with all dinner. I asked if she would like to come back to my apartment for a real drink. I didn't expect much more than a request to take her home.
"Sure," she said. "Why not."

*   *   *   *   *

As I unlocked the door to my quarters at the BOQ and we entered into the tiny foyer which led into the kitchen, I said beer was the preferred drink for me and my colleagues, but I did have one bottle of red wine and some rum in a cabinet below the sink. Beer, she said, would be fine. I opened two and we moved to my living room where I offered her the sofa and took a seat in the armchair opposite. We continued trying to explore the limited ground we'd plowed during dinner and, as we each finished our bottle of beer, the air of anticipatory awkwardness did begin to dissipate a bit. I moved from my chair to a position alongside her on the sofa. She seemed barely aware of the change in venue, but when I slipped my left arm behind her neck, she dropped her head toward the back of the sofa and we kissed. When we broke it off, she smiled warmly and we kissed again.

I followed with my next tentative move, slipping my right hand across her blouse and softly caressing her breast through the layers of fabric. She looked at me quizzically, took hold of my hand and removed it. I dropped it back into my lap. She turned and stared at me a moment, then smiled. When I started to say something, she put her index finger against my lips. "Ssshhh," she whispered, then unbuttoned her blouse, peeled it off, slipped her hands around her back and unhooked her bra, exposing her beautiful, youthful breasts. She then retrieved my hand and returned it to the breast I had been caressing.

"There, that's better," she said. "Don't you agree?"

Our eyes met. Again the warm smile. I was beside myself with anticipation.

Fully naked, the curves of her body were as sensual as I'd anticipated. And oh, she knew how to do this: where she put her hands, where she put her mouth, how she directed me toward her sex, then kissed me hard just as I pushed to enter her. It was all too much. I was already one thrill ahead before I was fully inside her. What should have been my post-coital embarrassment, however, did not have time to materialize as she reached up and took me by the shoulders, pulled me down hard atop her and kissed me again, as if she were trying to swallow me with her wide-open mouth.

Moving to the comfort of my bed, we made love twice more that night. She took more command each time, her facial expressions growing in intensity, almost dissociated from whatever sexual act we were engaged in south of the deep connection of her eyes with mine. It was as if she were searching for whatever hidden secrets she could discover, laid bare by my nakedness, exposed by the lack of any barriers between us, while we engaged each other there in my bed. My response, to whatever her expectations may have been, was simply to find ways to pleasure her. Within the embrace of this beautiful intimacy, it all came so naturally, so easy to do.

Words, freed of the awkwardness earlier in the evening, played no role now. It all wound to a conclusion, a détente of sorts, with both of us lying there on our backs, staring up at the ceiling, well past midnight. Exhausted, I said, finally, "I get up in five hours for our monthly parade formation."

She rolled toward me, rose up on an elbow and kissed me lightly on the lips. Then she said, "I don't go on duty until five this evening, captain." She smiled her crooked smile, rolled over and up onto her feet, then headed for the sofa in living room to retrieve her clothes. "I need to take a little more of your sleep time for a lift home, so I suggest you throw on some clothes. The highway cops around here don't like it when my dates drive me home stark naked."

* * * * *

Thus it began. Aldina and I spent every spare moment of time together. When we were apart, all I thought about was being naked with her. One Saturday, we had sex four times, sandwiched around and between a trip to the base theatre and dinner at a Mexican restaurant downtown. Each time, she participated with an intensity that pushed our lovemaking into dizzying territory that, beyond the pleasure it all delivered, puzzled me. During our lovemaking, she was a different person from the woman she was when we were doing anything else.

My days became a matter of marking time until I could get together with Aldina. Nonetheless, my duties on the flight line ate up most of my waking hours. Except for the colonel, who was chief of maintenance, most of the other officers charged with maintaining the aircraft, were junior to me, early in their tours. The only other officer I developed any kind of friendship with seemed the most unlikely of choices. He was also a captain, in charge of the engine repair facility, named Jim Lawler. A native New Mexican, he grew up in Silver City, in the western part of the state, about as far removed from New York City as any place could be, culturally as well as geographically. He, like me, was toward the end of his tour and had been at Cannon for all of it, since the need to train pilots for combat missions became more pressing as the war in Vietnam became more expansive through the '60s. Our friendship grew out of Lawler's good-naturedly mocking my New York accent, while I began to point out how he was starting to adopt some of my New York-ese phrases into his everyday speech. The other thing, which grew our friendship, was that Jim had started dating a girl from town named Kathy Johnson, whose father owned the local Ford dealership. I felt double dating with Jim and Kathy might add a bit of social context to my time with Aldina.

As I began to realize that the intense physical attraction was obscuring evidence that I was falling in love with Aldina, I started taking a more studied interest in her past and how it might shape her future with me. What she began to reveal about her family history was not pleasant. Her parents had divorced when she was five. They'd never had much of a marriage. Her mother, Rose Lopez, had conceived after a night of drink-induced passion with Tom Connor, the man who would become Aldina's father. It was just before he went off to war with the US Navy, as a salvage diver stationed in war-torn Italy during World War II. Too many tequilas had come at the end of a particularly bad day for Rose. She slept with Tom because of some unsettling news she had had about her true love, who was with the Marines, fighting in the Pacific.

Rose and Billy Smith had been sweethearts since freshman year at Clovis High School. After Billy left for the war in the Pacific, Rose pined for him ceaselessly. She lived for his letters. But after a year, he'd stopped writing. A dozen of her letters went unanswered, until she finally gave up writing them. During that period, his family was evasive when she pressed them as to why he'd stopped writing. Was he a prisoner of war? Was he even still alive? She needed to tell herself there had to be some compelling reason why he had stopped writing. Finally, his mother said Billy had married a girl he'd met on leave in Hawaii and would be moving with her to California after the war, where his new wife had some family.

That night, after fending off the local bar drunks, Rose slept with Tom, the guy who'd been buying her last several rounds. He seemed like the least offensive one and his come-ons were respectful. Soon pregnant and unmarried, Rose knew that during this prehistoric era for women, walking around with a

42

widening girth, she had better have a gold ring on her finger in a small town like Clovis. So she married this man for whom she had no real affection, then spent the four years while Tom was gone despondent over the one-time love of her life, with only the occasional thought of her absent stand-in husband. Tom wrote her religiously; Rose answered his letters sporadically.

"She had so poisoned the well," Aldina told me, "that the only thoughts I had of my daddy were that he was a bad man fighting other bad men."

"That's about the most simplistic over-simplification of the war I've ever heard," I replied.

"She told me that in the 1940s, Navy divers wore those bulky, weighted suits, with just a tiny round window on the front of the helmet in order to see what they were doing. They were hooked up to a pump on a surface vessel, monitored by a sailor who was dodging enemy planes as much as watching over the pump. My dad returned with stories of bullets whizzing through the sea next him, but too busy pulling bodies from sunken ships to worry about whether the seaman at the pump was still alive and the machinery might soon be shutting down and cutting off his air supply."

"So, while he was pulling bodies from sunken ships, she . . .

"She was screwing around on him. A lot. I was just a baby and had no idea these guys going in and out of her bedroom weren't my real 'uncles.' But, as a toddler, you know when there is no real affection for you. That you are just in the way. My daddy, though, he loved me from the moment we first saw each other. I had just turned four when he came home and into my life, but my first memory of him was reacting to his warm smile, running and jumping into his arms as he swept me up and gave me a kiss."

Badly affected by his war experiences, Tom Connor returned home a hopeless alcoholic.

"His eyeballs were floating, every day by noon," Aldina said. "While my mother made a decent salary as a receptionist at the bank, daddy couldn't hold a job for more than a month or two, even if it was just pumping gas or sweeping out the grade school

cafeteria. He spent almost all of what little he earned on booze.
My mother reacted by mocking him mercilessly until he would
fly into a rage. She seemed to take a masochistic pleasure in
provoking him to violence."

"That must have been brutal for you?"

"Of course, but *he* was the person who was always very kind
to me. He called me 'Alley Girl, *his* 'Little Alley Girl,' as if being
with me, cuddling with me were some kind of good place where
he could go for an escape from his world. He bought me things –
candy and toys – took me to dude ranches for pony rides, made
me feel loved. It was a feeling I'd not experienced before, not
much from my mother, and certainly not from her trail of lovers,
who wanted nothing to do with me."

A year after Tom's return from the war, Rose spent most of
her savings on a divorce lawyer, took her young daughter and
headed to Los Angeles where she had a sister who said she could
get her into a training program with the phone company there.
Leaving her father behind took from Aldina the only love she
was experiencing and replaced it with a deep sense of loss. Her
father had neither the funds nor the resume to mount any kind
of opposition to Rose's moves. When Rose permitted Aldina to
say good-bye to her father, she rushed into his arms and cried,
holding on as if for dear life, until her father released his grip
and she was pulled from his arms.

"I felt I was leaving behind me that warm feeling I got with
him and the only place I would ever be able to find it again."

In California, Rose devoted a good deal of her free time
trying to locate the lover who had jilted her. Eventually, a name
and address from phone company records revealed a Billy
Smith, driving distance from where Rose lived with her sister.
She borrowed her sister's car, drove to the address on a
weekend, rang the doorbell and a woman answered. The
woman called her husband to the door, but he was a frumpy
couch potato, who bore no resemblance to her former lover,
even accounting for any added weight and some aging.

"Really, Rose," one of her coworkers replied when she described the encounter. "You think some guy named William Smith, living in the LA area, is your long lost love?"

"Not William," she replied. "His name was Billy. That's why I thought . . ."

No other leads ever turned up another Billy Smith. Rose finally realized that the story his parents had told her about his moving to California was probably just a lie to keep her from ever locating him.

By the time Aldina was in her early teens, her mother had begun dating a man who owned a used car lot. Rose had finally saved enough to buy a car. She was still a looker and Chuck Spencer, the car lot owner, came on to her as soon as she walked into his office to inquire about a five-year-old, blue Chevy Malibu. She was soon spending almost every night at his house and did that for the better part of a year, until Rose told Chuck without a wedding ring she would not be coming over any more. They were married by a justice of the peace, then Rose and Aldina moved in. Almost immediately, Chuck began suggestive moves toward Aldina. He took to walking down the hall each night and quietly pushing the door open to her room, staring inside for a seeming eternity, then moving on.

"I woke up one night to find his hand down my pajama bottoms. I pulled it away and was about to scream, when he slapped the other hand over my mouth, and stared down at me with a look that could kill. I got little sleep my final year in high school. I was determined to get the hell out of there, but the only place I could think of to run to was back here to Clovis."

"You had your father here."

She fell quiet. Then finally, "A couple of months after we left for California, he got very drunk one night and rolled his car over and down into an arroyo. He died of a broken neck. I don't think I'm making too much of it to say what really was broken was his heart."

"I'm so sorry, Aldina."

"Anyway, I was a big Janis Joplin fan at the time. It created a bit of a rebellious spirit in me. I started dressing like her; got big, round glasses, bangles around my neck and hanging from my ears, let my hair grow long and crazy. It attracted one of the high school tough guys and we started dating. I had some ridiculous sense he could somehow protect me from Chuck. But I spent most of my time protecting myself from him. Pushing him off took all my determination and sometimes most of my strength. Finally, I just gave up and let him take my virginity. It turns out that was all he ever wanted from me. He bragged to everyone about it. I had to spend most of my remaining time in high school trying to keep my distance from him. None of the other guys wanted to touch me. They were afraid of him. Besides any of the so-called decent guys considered me damaged goods. If I'd had any thoughts of staying in LA, he ruined it for me. Him and fuckin' Chuck."

Again, "I'm sorry, Aldina," was all I could muster.

"The day after I graduated from high school," she continued, "I headed back here to live with an aunt, Ginny, my father's older sister, and her husband, uncle Ralph. Aunt Ginny knew how much my father loved me and was happy to take me in. My mother put up no resistance when I told her I'd been accepted at Eastern New Mexico University. She'd always viewed me as excess baggage, the kid she'd had by accident with some guy she never loved."

Aldina said she'd stayed in touch with her aunt during her years in California and as she approached her graduation from high school, her aunt wrote that she could get Aldina into college as a resident if she moved in with her aunt and uncle and because she had been born in New Mexico. After she relocated, Aldina took an array of courses at ENMU, but only the acting class had any appeal for her.

"A year later," she said, "I met you at the movie theatre."

*　*　*　*　*

She gave me more details over the next several times we met, as if she wanted to make sure I knew about the woman with whom I was getting more and more involved.

"There was nothing in my past to indicate I'd want to do anything like acting, except maybe for one trip to Disneyland when I was six and wishing I could be Snow White or the princess in Sleeping Beauty. But once I got into the class, I loved it."

We were sitting at a table behind the bachelor officers' quarters, finishing up a steak I'd grilled on the barbecue on the patio.

"I took a drama class at ENMU," Aldina was saying. "Hell, I don't know why. But the professor who taught the class was very encouraging. One of those times in your life when you feel like you may have found out about something you didn't know you had in you."

"One of those times in your life? You're not even twenty. How many 'one of those timeses' can you have had?"

"Well," she replied, "I had *this* 'one of those times.' What, you've never had any?"

"Touché. Early on in school, I was pushed toward science and math. You know, guy things. And I was good at those classes, really good. Since I was the first member of my family likely to make it into college, my father was determined I be an engineer or some kind of scientist. It's not like he was ordering me to, or anything like that. He just kept trying to convince me that was where I would make a real good life for myself and my future family. And, I was good enough at those subjects to make MIT as a chemistry major. But once I got there, it was the humanities courses I gravitated toward. It was just one of those times. You know what I mean?"

She just smiled. We'd had a couple of beers.

"I felt I had little choice," I continued, "but to move back to New York City and transfer to writing courses at NYU. My father resisted at first, but then supported my move. Once I was editor of the student newspaper, he read everything I wrote."

"May *I* continue?" she asked.

I nodded.

"My professor had taught drama classes at community colleges around LA before coming here," she said. "He'd sent some of his students to audition for parts at the Hollywood studios. He had framed letters from some of the studios on the wall of his classroom. He was always pointing them out to us.”

She paused and took a breath, a kind of fluttering breath.

“Somehow, I’m not getting a good vibe off your tone here,” I offered.

She shook her head. “His interest in me was just a come-on. He tells me he can give me some one-on-one coaching at his apartment, which he can’t do with his course load at school. Of course, I knew what he wanted by asking me there, but he had convinced me I had some raw talent and I at least had to try to develop it.”

“The world is full of scumbags, like him” I said. “I mean who on a career path in movies, theatre or TV goes from LA to Portales, New Mexico? There must have been some misdeeds involved.”

“I’m sure. But who goes from Portales, New Mexico to Hollywood without some help? *I* wouldn’t have much of a career path *here*, so I knew what I wanted from him, too.”

I lowered my gaze and shook my head.

“What?” she asked.

“What *you* wanted from *him*?”

“Problem?”

“How Machiavellian.”

“What the hell are you talking about, Michael?”

“Never mind.”

“No,” she replied. What the hell *are* you talking about?”

“Then, what about me?” I asked.

“Somehow this is about you?”

“What did you want from me?”

She was quiet a moment, then smiled. “Oh, OK,” she said. She paused a moment, then, “you know, it’s strange. Now that you ask, no, I *didn’t* have a plan for you.”

“Strange? No plan?”

Her smiled broadened. “You were so sweet. So unsure of what you were doing to get my attention. Like a teenager asking

a new girl out for his first date. I wanted to see how it would
play out."

"Play out? Just one of your improv scenes?"

"I guess." She stared at me a while. Her smile grew warmer.
"I don't really know. I don't think I was thinking anything
beyond just going out with you. I don't know if I'd ever really
had that experience before. No game plan, I mean."

"Well, let the record show, *I* didn't have a game plan."

"Oh, come on, Mike. You take me to the O Club, where I fit in
like a sheep at a gathering of wolves?"

"I didn't know where else to take you."

"You didn't take me there to impress me?"

"Of course I did. And it worked, right?"

"Define 'worked.'"

I just smiled.

"Then you ask me back to your place?"

"OK, you win," I replied. "But let's just say our first date was
. . . memorable."

She looked at me quizzically. "Memorable?"

"Lovely?"

"Memorable and lovely?"

"Why not?" I said. "Writer's words, perhaps?"

"How about hot?" she countered. "The word of a would-be
actress, then. How about 'hot'?"

"OK, check that box. Hot."

"Whatever. But it's what you wanted, right?"

"It's what every guy wants."

"Yes, so I needed to get on with it, then."

"Get on with it? Is that what we did? Just get on with it?

"We're here ain't we?"

I shook my head. "I'm sorry, *I* wasn't just getting on with it.
Hot, yes, but memorable because it was lovely. They may be
simply writer's words, but for me they describe how I felt. How
I feel. You caught me completely off-guard that first night. And
yes, it did start off hot, but for me, it turned lovely. After you left,
all I could think about was I had made love to a beautiful young
woman and for me it was . . . lovely."

"Do you always hammer away at a point until the other person gives?"

I sat without words for a moment, then, "Aldina," I said, "I love you."

She stared at me a moment, her eyebrows scrunching, then she nodded. "OK," she replied, "I give."

*   *   *   *   *

As my final year in the service wound toward its close, the war overseas continued to escalate. The need for our base to crank out combat-trained pilots became more intense. Pilots and ground staff were deployed for their yearlong tours of duty in Vietnam, spaced out in three-month intervals, so we would have a controlled turnover of the four squadrons on our base between those coming to us from flight school and those leaving us for combat duty. Most of those who returned from the warzone stayed with us for ninety days to reacclimate before heading to combat-ready stateside bases and to remain prepared to return to active combat duty if and when necessary. A few got permanent assignments on our base to take up instructor pilot roles.

This dynamic made for all kinds of creative inspiration for me to somehow maintain the writing skills I'd developed in college, while I paced a flight line making sure the airplanes remained flight ready. I kept journals about how men reacted to getting ready to go fight in a foreign land, and the possibility they would die there. I made notes on how their experiences may have changed them when they'd actually strafed armies of other men or napalmed villages where women and children, old men and old women were incinerated. Those of us who were stateside players getting the warriors prepped, were mere corner men for the fighters in the center of the ring.

I filled journals with my observations. Real life beings in those journals would sometimes morph into characters slipping from my notes to become players in partially written stories or

lines in free-verse poetry. But more and more Aldina was
becoming the principal subject of my writing:

> Aldina, what's become of your life.
> You search and search for answers,
> Strung like beads that burrow through your ears.
> You sip the nectar of daylight,
> Then embrace the shadows of the night
> And . . . and . . .

No matter how often I played with story lines, lines of
poetry, even lyrics in partially written songs, the paragraphs, the
couplets, the stanzas were filaments in some lamp of expression,
which somehow could not glow to full candescence. The
sentences, the lines, the *whatever*, read as if they *were* complete,
but didn't proceed to what I really wanted to say or how I really
wanted to say it. I would struggle to find the best words, but it
was as if the language didn't contain them. After each time
Aldina and I met, each time we talked, each time we made love,
lines would begin to flow like free verse poetry, but peter out
before ever arriving at some sort of stasis, a jumbled succession
of scenes that never led to the right ending.

With the close of our third month together, Aldina missed
her period. During all our weeks together, I had become so
obsessed with having sex with her I avoided focusing on the
responsible things to do, or at the very least the responsible
questions to ask. It was really a deflection to assume that she
had done what she needed to do to protect herself and I didn't
want to go down any road that would stop her from going to bed
with me. Now there was the very real possibility that she would
bear a child of mine. When that very real possibility was staring
me in the face . . . I couldn't look at her without musing about
what having babies with her would be like. I found it nothing
but pleasing. After dinner one night at my apartment, I got
down on one knee and asked her to marry me. The penetrating
look that had become so concerning to me, melted into a
softness. She leaned down, slipped an arm around my neck and

nodded. Our former acrobatic lovemaking, that night, softened
into a warmth I'd not experienced before with her. I couldn't
help but feel, for the first time in my life, I was experiencing
what real love feels like.

"I love you, Aldina," I said as we lay in each other's arms.

She lifted her head and placed it onto my chest. "You too,
captain," she replied.

* * * * *

I flew with her to New York, where we spent the weekend at
my family's home. Aldina didn't say much, had difficulty
interacting with my ever-embracing relatives, then seemed
relieved when it was time to leave. My mother made it apparent
that she was unimpressed but tried as best she could to
sublimate her feelings that I was rushing into something I hadn't
really thought through. But she never directly said so. Instead,
she just talked all around it.

"She doesn't wear shoes much," my mother said, when she
and I were one-on-one. It was as if she needed to find some
reason to tell me I hadn't thought this through without coming
right out an saying it.

"Doesn't wear shoes? She's not some hick farm girl, mom," I
said, in response to the inference of her comment. "She's from
California. It's a beach look out there."

"Well, it's just something I noticed." My mother looked at me
a while. It seemed as if she wanted to shake her head, but
couldn't bring herself to do even that.

While I never told my family Aldina was pregnant, I'm sure
they suspected that was driving my decision. Before Aldina and
I left to head to the airport for our return flights, my father
pulled me aside and slipped me a hundred dollars. He told me to
pay for at least some part of our wedding rings with the money
so that every time we looked at the rings we would know that he
had wished us a lifetime of love. It brought a tear to my eye. I
shook his hand and we hugged tightly.

"You bring your Dee-Dee-Deena home soon," he said, when
we broke apart, "and we'll make sure she knows she's family."

"Your father is a very sweet man," Aldina told me on the flight back to New Mexico. "He reminds me of my father."

"Does he, now, Dee-Dee-Deena?"

She just smiled at me.

The hundred dollars paid for the two plain gold wedding rings I bought and we were married by the chaplain at Cannon. The only other attendees at our wedding were Aldina's Aunt Ginny and Uncle Ralph, along with Jim Lawler and Kathy Johnson. Aldina made no mention of whether she had even told her mother.

*　*　*　*　*

Once we had returned to Cannon, I was hoping for a resumption of the play we were starring in before all the recent dramatic turns. On the upside, Kathy Johnson's father, the Ford dealer, had made me a terrific deal on the trade-in of my four-year-old Plymouth Satellite for a 1967 powder-blue Thunderbird convertible. It had belonged to a young lieutenant from Wisconsin, who had driven it little while at Cannon and didn't want it to be sitting out in the bitterly cold Midwest winter, while he spent a year in the steaming jungles of Southeast Asia. The lieutenant had taken a beating selling it back and that translated into a great deal for me.

I found every excuse to drive the T-Bird anywhere. A beautiful Saturday afternoon, with just a hint of a breeze, was begging for a ride downtown with the top down in my new car and to show off my new wife. We were sitting in the parking lot of Tastee Freez taking our last licks of two chocolate cones, when a young man headed in our direction. He was nattily dressed in a perfectly fitted open-neck, long sleeve blue shirt and perfectly creased beige pants.

"Oh gawd," Aldina said as he approached the car.

"What?" I said, noting her concern. "Is he gonna be a problem?"

"Don't worry," she replied.

"Don't worry?"

"He's a weenie."

"Aldina?" the man said as he came up to us, stopping along the passenger side of the T-Bird. "You're latest conquest?" He flashed a phony smile in my direction.

"Excuse me?" I said and started to continue, but Aldina cut me off.

"You referring to my husband, are you?"

"Oh," he replied. "Respectability. Finally."

Again I started to say something, but again she cut me off.

"Captain," she said, "at Cannon. Real man not a character you play in an Enemy U theatre production, Bobby Gee Junior."

His phony smile turned to a scowl.

"Look," I said holding up my left hand and starting the engine with my right. "We need to move on before this turns ugly."

"You had your one pass at the better gene pool," he shouted as we pulled away.

"Better gene pool?" I said as we turned onto US 60 and headed back toward Cannon.

"Hardly," she replied. "Wasn't even a decent one-night stand."

"Excuse me?" I said, launching a hard look in her direction.

"Oh, come on, Mike," she said, "I did have a life before I met you."

I looked over at her and shook my head. "Well, at least you did end up in the better gene pool. What the hell was that all about?"

"I took an acting class with him. We had an assignment to create some dialog around a budding romance and perform it together. That seemed to work so well we started dating, until I found out all he was good at was acting. He's an arrogant bastard. His father is the bank president. He's Robert George Henderson, Junior. Hated it when I christened him 'Bobby Gee Junior,' and all his in-crowd friends started calling him that.'"

I just shook my head again, but couldn't stifle a laugh.

"Forget about him, sweetheart," she said. "My past life."

"Sweetheart?"

I cranked up the music full blast. She smiled one of those smiles I had come to live for and let the pleasantly warm, dry air slipping over the windshield play with her hair all the way back to the base.

*　*　*　*　*

Given how little time I had left in the service, Base Housing moved us into a two-bedroom unit, furnished with the barest of essentials, most left by other officers, who had been reassigned. I continued with my routine on the flight line each day. She had little to do beyond TV soap operas during the day and brief chats with other wives along the loop where we lived. After dinner in the evenings, we watched mostly TV sitcoms. We had no friends beyond Jim Lawler and Kathy Johnson, so we played cards with them a couple of nights each week, occasionally catching a movie at the base theatre pretty much each time they changed the featured presentation.

As Aldina's pregnancy moved forward, her morning sickness became particularly hard and her near persistent discomfort made her irritable. Her condition further limited any outside contact to no more than the card games with Jim and Kathy. This forced confinement did not sit well with Aldina and she seemed to be in foul moods continually. I dealt with her surliness by drowning it in more alcohol. Sessions with our two friends degenerated into Jim and me drinking more and more heavily and the card games becoming less relevant. I felt I'd have some measure of relief when we got home to New York and we would have family to help us.

We'd decided that it would be best for Aldina to fly to New York two weeks before my discharge, rather than taking the two thousand mile drive across country in the T-Bird. She'd set up in a spare bedroom at my parent's house, where she could have daily looking-after and begin to get to know the family better. The morning after the movers had finished packing our meager personal belongings and the apartment had passed an inspection by Base Housing, I put Clovis in the rearview mirror shortly after dawn, hoping to make the east Texas piney woods by sundown and forever trade beige arroyos and red-dust storms for a welcome palette of greens. Arriving in New York, after four days on the road, I found Aldina had not made much of a connection with family. She was having a particular problem with my mother's dictatorial control of just about everything and no amount of my father's tenderness was having any beneficial counter effect.

I immediately began a search for work to replace my Air Force captain's pay. I spent most of my time applying for jobs in journalism, but New York had lost four of its seven daily newspapers while I was in the Air Force and four years in aircraft maintenance did not serve me well for positions at newspapers or magazines. I finally got an entry-level position at a PR agency. I hated the work so I spent nights writing pitch letters for freelance writing assignments, but having no luck with any of those.

Four weeks after my return to New York, Aldina miscarried and within days of that started to develop signs of postpartum depression. She had unpredictable mood swings, from sadness to anxiety to feeling overwhelmed with the new urban landscape of New York, so different from the dusty New Mexico plateau or even the casualness of Los Angeles. She had persistent insomnia and trouble eating, insisting the latter was a result of the differences between the southwestern diet she had grown up with versus the European influences I was accustomed to. Anti-depressant drugs mitigated the problems somewhat, but not enough to make life tolerable for her, let alone for me. Finally, she informed me that she needed a change of venue, to spend some time in her comfort zone, to try to regain some semblance of her former self.

"I called Aunt Ginny today and asked if I could come and spend a couple of weeks with her and Uncle Ralph to get past the depression of losing my baby," she said.

"Of losing our baby," I replied.

"Of course, Aunt Ginny said, 'yes.' She's always been there for me."

"Really?" I replied. "Come on. You'll get past all that here . . .
with me. The doctor said you'll get over this. It'll just take a little
more time."

"What's a little more time? It's been weeks now and I don't
see any improvement. I'm driving you and everyone here crazy
and that's not helping me to recover. I need to do this, Michael.
I need to do this for me and for you."

"I'll miss you terribly," I said. "We've seldom been apart
since we met."

"I know," she replied. "So maybe we both need some time
apart."

"I'll miss you."

"Jesus, Mike," she said. "I'll just be with Aunt Ginny and
Uncle Ralph. I'm not defecting to Russia."

And so, she left.

*　*　*　*　*

It felt good to see Jim Lawler, again. He was in New York for
a convention of Ford dealers. Discharged shortly after me, he
and Kathy had married and opted to make their home in Clovis,
where Jim now worked with Kathy's father as the second in
command at the Ford dealership. He was trying to convince the
old man to expand the business by taking a larger role in
corporate and industry functions.

We met for a round of drinks at the Oyster Bar in Grand
Central Terminal. After the opening pleasantries, I told him that
I hadn't seen Aldina for almost three months. I'd written her
and called asking when she was planning to return but each
time, she insisted that she needed more time to "work things out
in my head." When I said I was going there to bring her home,
she was emphatic that I not come. I insisted I would come
anyway. She said if I did, she'd avoid seeing me. She kept
insisting she needed more time to sort things out and that she
could only do that on her timetable. I'd told her I was nearing my
wits' end.

Jim said Kathy, had heard that Aldina had returned to Clovis
and was living with her aunt and uncle. He then alluded,

nervously, that they'd found out some other things about what she'd been up to.

"I wasn't sure how much contact you've had with her," he said.

"As I've said not that much," I replied, "and what I have had has not gone well. I feel like she's writing me off."

"I guess she feels more at home in Clovis," Jim answered.

"I'm not sure she feels at home anywhere," I said, "but for some reason, she is always drawn back to that God-damned windblown plateau. No offense, James. I see you're carving out a good living there."

"No offense taken," he said. "Clovis has grown, even in the half-year since you left. The oil and gas business in west Texas has been migrating our way and bringing a good deal of money with it."

"Nice," I replied. "So, you were saying?"

He didn't respond but sat there twiddling with the stirrer from his drink.

"What is it?" I asked finally.

He let out a sigh. "She's working at The PoleKitten."

The comment took a moment to register, then, "Really?" I said. "She waitressing? I know she's not bartending. She doesn't know squat about mixing drinks."

He just stared at me without saying a word.

Then. "No," I said.

"Unfortunately, yes."

"You sure?"

"Would I say something like that if I wasn't sure?"

"Wonderful."

"I felt I had to check it out," he continued. "Kathy wasn't thrilled. I mean I'm somewhat of a man of importance around town. 'Can't you wear a disguise?' she said, when she finally agreed to let me go. 'Beard, moustache, something like that?'"

I just shook my head.

"When I walked in," he continued, "Aldina was sitting at a table in the back of the room. She had a sweater draped over her shoulders, but otherwise was, to put in nicely, scantily clad. You know."

Again, I just shook my head.

"She paid me no mind as I walked over toward her. 'Aldina?' I said. She looked up at me, gave me a quick onceover, then went back to her drink."

"Oh, come on," I offered. "She knows you. You sure it was her."

He ignored my comment. "I stood there a while longer, then went and sat down at a table not far from the stage. I'd glance back at her from time to time, while the girl on stage went through her gyrations. Aldina just stared down at her drink as if . . ."

"What?"

"As if she couldn't bear to have me know she'd recognized me."

A sadness swept over me.

"As if she didn't want someone, who knew her when, to . . ."

"To what?"

"Who knew her when she could lift her head with some measure of dignity."

I looked at him a while and shook my head. "Jesus, Jim. Life hasn't played all that fairly with her."

He looked at me a moment, then receded to staring down at his drink. "The last I saw of her was when she got up from the table and headed toward the stage. As she passed my table, she said, 'Dinner, Jim? At the O Club? Maybe this time they'll let me have a drink at the bar.'"

I dropped my head and stared at my knotted fingers in my lap. I was bereft of words.

Jim drained his drink and got up. "Good seeing ya, good buddy," he said. "You hang in there, you know. You'll get past this."

"Thanks" was all I could muster.

"Well," he replied, "at least she finally got to perform on stage."

"Hey!" I snapped. "That's my wife you're talking about. She's my wife, God dammit."

He shook his head. "I'll get the drinks," he said and walked off toward the bar to pay the check.

*   *   *   *   *

The pilot of the Trans Texas Airlines flight out of Dallas was having a bitch of a time struggling with unpredictable crosswinds, as he battled to maintain final approach into Amarillo Airport. Fighter pilots at Cannon derided TTA as "Tree Top Airlines," but I doubted any of them would have done better at bringing our turboprop down safely. During my four years in the Air Force, there'd only been a couple of times when I'd wanted to kiss the ground after landing from a particularly harrowing flight. By the time we had touched down and the pilot had wobbled our aircraft to the terminal, this flight had made it onto that short list.

Through the terminal windows, I could see the ominous red layer floating atop the dusty beige landscape, with tiny wind eddies dancing in an otherwise crystal-clear blue sky. For most of the hundred-mile drive from Amarillo to Clovis, my rental car was buffeted in the terra-firma variation of the aircraft dance, but at least in this version they would pull my injured body from my upside-down vehicle, instead of my charred remains from the aircraft wreckage. Ah, I thought, springtime in Clovis.

I had hours to kill in a town, which not that long ago had had meaning for me, albeit most of the positive meaning involving Aldina. At least it once did. There were Jim and Kathy, of course, but after my encounter with Jim in New York, I didn't want to see him again. By early evening, the winds had died down, so I just got into my rental car and drove down to the ENMU campus in Portales and wandered around directionless for a while, had a burger at a McDonalds near the school, then headed back to my hotel and spent the hours until night had firmly settled in, watching mindless TV, nearly overcome by an intense sense of loneliness, until it was time to go.

During the drive to The PoleKitten, my hands were literally shaking holding the steering wheel; the rest of my body was quaking as if I had the chills. Once through the doors, it was like an out-of-body experience as I chose a seat in the back of the room. I lost all track of time as I watched a parade of young females caressing a metal pole in a dance that had lost any vestige of eroticism for me. I nursed a succession of slowly consumed beers, but even a mild buzz was not helping as much as I had hoped.

Late in the cavalcade of dancers, the PA finally boomed, "All right, boys, as we like to say, wouldn't you like to meet *her* down an alley. Ooooh, yeah. The PoleKitten is proud to present, our very own alley kitten, the one, the only, Alley Girl."

I winced in dismayed expectation. She came strutting out onto the stage, a spotlight following her to the pole. I felt violated as she slid behind the gleaming metal pole, wrapped her right leg around it and, as she stared out toward the audience, crooned, "How you doin', cowboys?"

There were whoops and whistles and a barrage of crude comments.

"Now, boys, you –"

And then our eyes met.

"Good to see y'all," she said, her voice fluttering.

Even with me a distance from her, she in the spotlight, me in muted light, a connection was instantly reestablished.

"I . . ." she stuttered. "I . . ." Suddenly, she slid down from the pole, turned and walked swiftly across the stage and disappeared behind a curtain.

There were hoots and boos, patrons stomping the floor.

A new performer was quickly shuffled out onto the stage. She was greeted with louder boos and hoots, shouts of "Alley Kitten!" "Bring back Alley Girl!"

The substitute performer began a succession of more and more leud gestures and the audience began to settle into the performance.

A man emerged from behind the stage and walked directly toward my table.

"Sir," he said standing before me, "I'm afraid I'm going to have to ask you to leave."

"What?" I replied.

"You need to leave. You're upsetting one of my performers."

"Now how can that be? I'm not intoxicated or disruptive. I've done nothing but sit here, quietly, without uttering a word."

I noted one of the bouncers having moved to a position closer to my table. "Really? You're going to have me bounced out of here for sitting quietly at my table?"

"Nevertheless, you're upsetting one of my performers."

"One of your 'performers' is my wife," I said, for the first time raising my voice. Some of the patrons nearby turned and stared in our direction.

The comment seemed to take him by surprise. He stared hard at me but said nothing.

"Didn't she tell you that?" I asked.

His eyebrows furrowed as he continued to study me.

"Tell ya what," I said. "Have her throw on some clothes and come talk to me. When we're done talking, I'll leave. Quietly. You won't have any problem with me, after that."

He studied me a moment longer, then turned and retreated toward the stage.

I sat staring blankly at the young woman, almost totally naked, now. She might as well have been, for me, nothing more than a tiny hill of New Mexico red dust on some windowsill.

When the man returned, he said, "She'll see you out back. We have a picnic table there. Go out the front door, then down the alley to the back of the theatre."

"She'll be there when I get there, right?" I questioned, sternly.

"She'll be there."

Aldina was sitting on one of the attached benches at a wooden picnic table just in front of the black metal rear stage door. She was wearing a modified version of one of her Janis Joplin looks: a loose-fitting dress, a long, loopy necklace and the oversized glasses she had on the first time I saw her at the movie theatre.

"Hello, Mike," she said. "As you can see, I've finally made it on stage."

"Yes, I see that," I said, as I sat on the bench opposite. "I didn't mean to upset your performance when you came out. I just wanted to have a talk with you."

"Well," she said. "Here we are."

"What's going on with you?" I asked. "I really do want to help."

"Help?"

"Yes, understand what you need, then take you home."

"Home? Where's that?"

"Well, it's not here."

She gave me a quizzical look.

"Here?" I questioned. "You think *this* is home?"

"I didn't fit in in New York, Michael. You're different people, where you come from."

"What? Too big city? You've lived in LA."

"Yeah," she said, "and we know how that worked out."

"You didn't have *me* in LA, Aldina. You didn't have me to love you in LA."

She looked at me warmly. "I know, Michael. I know."

We were quiet for a few moments. Then she said, "I've gone back to college."

"At Enemy U?"

"E.N.M.U., Mike." She pronounced each letter as if the initials had taken on more-esteemed significance. "The drama program again."

"So then, you're interning here at The PoleKitten?"

"The money's good and it pays for my classes and books."

"Aren't you worried one or more of those A-holes in the audience will do you some real harm? Will follow you home?"

"One of the bouncers picks me up and drives me home."

"The perks of star billing?"

"The perks."

I just shook my head. "So then, what do we do, you and me?"

She let out a deep breath and lowered her head. "I've found someone," she said.

"Found someone?"

"He's the new drama program professor. Young man. They got rid of that other asshole. Terry, is a graduate of the program at the college. He's from around here and he's creating a local theatre company. We see a lot of things the same way."

"But, Aldina, you are *my* wife."

"He and I want to see if we can make it together," she said, as if what I'd said had lost any meaning.

"O.K., let's go with this," I said. "When were you going to let me know?"

"Soon," she said, "soon."

I just shook my head.

"You're a sweetheart, Michael. I have nothing but warm feelings for you but we are from two different worlds. You could never live here in my world and I could never live there, in yours."

"I came here to take you to your home," I said. "With me."

"My home is here," she replied.

"You really mean that?" I asked. "You're sure? Because you are walking away from something really good."

"I know that, Mike. Don't you think I know that. But unless I start over, unless *we* start over it will be torture for both of us, until we end up doing this later on and after much bitterness. I don't want to go there, Michael. I don't want to put you through that."

"But I love you, Aldina."

"I know," she said averting her eyes. "I know you do."

"And?

She looked back at me. "And . . . what?"

I waited but she said nothing further.

Finally, I said, "Did I pass that test you kept making me take?

She took a breath, nodded her head softly, looked at me straight on and smiled warmly. "Yes," she said. "You did. Every time."

We sat silently for a few moments, as I dealt with the
sadness that was welling up inside me. Then, "O.K." I said. "O.K.
I'll have a lawyer draw up papers. An amicable divorce.
Amicable, as in among . . . friends?"

Her smile warmed further. "Friends, of course."

We sat in silence, again, then, "Well," she said.

"I know," I answered. "I . . . know."

She rose from her seat.   "Mike," she said, giving me the full
version of her crooked smile, "please don't stay for my show."

I just looked down at my hands and nodded. When I looked
up she was already disappearing behind the black metal stage
door.

We were bucking an uncharacteristic headwind on the flight
from Amarillo east toward Dallas, so much so the Trans Texas
pilot was on the intercom explaining the wind direction was
highly unusual and therefor would not be with us for long. I
looked up from the notes I'd been scribbling in one of my
notebooks. We experienced a bump or two more before settling
into smooth air for the rest of the flight. "There's a metaphor in
there somewhere," I mumbled, shook my head and smiled. My
seatmate looked at me quizzically. "It's a long story," I said and
went back to my notebook. The Dallas-to-New York leg was
uneventful.

*　*　*　*　*

Aldina was on a tumbling roll to find love. Each time she had
tried and failed, she developed an ingrained suspicion that she'd
never succeed at it. Ever. Any positive experience in her life had
had only an ephemeral existence, eventually revealed as
camouflaged to disguise her being used. When my love didn't
seem to fit this pattern, she could not accept that. She kept
probing for what she was sure would be revealed as just another
subterfuge. But she was wrong about me. My intensions were
always genuine. Nonetheless, she could not stop probing to
uncover evidence of my lack of true feelings for her. But how
could she search out negative space? She suffered all of this
despite what was unquestionably real: the sincerity of my love,

there from the outset, validated through our marriage, especially the love I lavished upon her after the loss of the child we would have had together. She was wrong about me. *Wrong* about me. And when she finally accepted that, she moved on. She had opened up to the possibility of love, but it would not be with me. Maybe my need to give her the love she needed was for *my* fulfillment.

So Aldina would dance around the stage at The PoleKitten, alluring patrons, with that irresistible body, that sexy crooked smile, seducing them to stuff bills down her G-string, hinting at possibilities that nonetheless would leave them unfulfilled walk-on/walk-offs in her life and leave me to head out to my next chapter, until I could no longer head out to . . .

I lay alone in my bed, the night I returned from Clovis, staring at the ceiling, the lines of the song just rolling around and around in my head:

> *It never rains. It never snows.*
> *That God-damned wind*
> *just blows and blows.*

That fuckin' wind just blows . . . and blows.

Warming temperatures in the southwest brought the westerly winds earlier that year, herding, then dispersing the tumbleweed in their unsuccessful search to find a place to drop their seeds, piling up along the walls of houses until there was no more vacant space to accommodate any more of them, the new arrivals rolling up the backs of those that had assembled earlier, then flying over the rooftops and moving on. But, that year, there were unusual weather patterns: an odd stillness of air and the occasional day when the winds blew hard out of the east. Forecasters could not remember a similar period when that had ever occurred.

&

There was no emotion in her voice. It was part of a setting that had grown so strange. My reaction to the flatness in her demeanor now was that somehow she had managed to get me to reveal who I was. This was supposed to be all about her . . . but now the story was about me. Somehow, she had managed to expose me as the lead character in my own story and definitely not a sympathetic one . . .

THAT LAST YEAR AT OLOFFSON'S

The first time I'd seen Gabby at the Grand Hotel Oloffson, I had come to Haiti for the annual pre-Lenten carnival with a good friend of mine who ran a successful advertising and public relations agency in Miami. Tom was mixing some business with a lot of pleasure. We had gone to college together. While we'd both had aspirations about being writers, Tom had decided to make writing pay. Now he had the money to play. He'd been winning at the casino in the Royal Haitian and giving it back to the ladies every night, Dominican women working the clubs for men who preferred their dark-eyed, light-chocolate-skinned, Latin look. Tom was one of those extremely gregarious personalities who usually found a way to command the center of any gathering.

I'd been doing ongoing research for the Haiti section I wrote in a Caribbean travel guide. I'd also managed to convince a European news service to give me an assignment on the carnival and the Haitian cultural experience. I'd given up trying to keep up with Tom, so I stayed behind, each night, to sort through my notes. The lingering sounds of the music from the street bands knifing through the tamarind trees in the garden on my side of the hotel played counterpoint to the solitude of my room, with its terrace overlooking the lights of Port-au-Prince at the base of the hill.

It was the early 1980s. I'd been writing travel articles for more than a decade by then and had some impressive exposure in the better travel magazines. When the editors for a new Caribbean travel guide were recruiting writers for the various sections, I'd sought and won the Dominican assignment. All the other assignments went rapidly, except for Haiti, the most impoverished country in the Western Hemisphere, with the added onus as a hotspot for the spread of HIV/AIDS. As a result, no one wanted to write the Haiti section in the guidebook. Since Haiti occupied the western portion of the island of Hispaniola, which it shared with the Dominican Republic, the guidebook editor assigned the country to me, despite my protests. "It's the same island," he'd said. "It's not like I can just drive over the border," I countered. "They hate each other. Hell, Dominican Independence Day marks the date the country freed itself from Haitian rule. I'd have to fly from the DR back to either Miami or New York to get back there." "You want to write for us or not?" he countered. I took the assignment. Thus, my journeys there became a deep dive into loneliness. Even the better hotels had few rooms occupied. Dinner at the better restaurants were often just me and perhaps one or two other patrons present. I dreaded going to the country.

Except for the Grand Hotel Oloffson. Named for the
Norwegian ship captain who had converted it from an ornate
Victorian property built for a former president of Haiti, the hotel
was operated by a surly expat New Yorker, who had a sign on
his desk which read, "The Customer Is Always Wrong."
Nonetheless, the guestbook of those who had stayed there read
like an A-list of celebrities and socialites. The guests who were
deemed worthy had one of the accommodations named after
him or her, according to the proprietor's opinion of their
worthiness, from the commodious Sir John Gielgud Suite to
Chambre Mick Jagger, the smallest room in the hotel.

Given its notoriety among the celebrated, Oloffson's became
a place frequented by a cast of pretenders to status, characters
out of a novel by Graham Greene, a short story by Somerset
Maugham, or even one by Hemingway. So, each time I stayed
there, I passed my depressively lonely nights before going to
bed, writing exercises in fiction, inspired by my observations of,
and strange encounters with, the bizarre characters who stayed
at the hotel, some of whom were regulars during carnival time.
This time, Tom was one of the colorful characters livening things
up, a significant element in my personal entertainment. And
then, there was Gabby.

Tom, of course, was the one who broke the ice with Gabby.
He and I had been dining at the restaurant on the veranda, when
she came up the stone steps from street level, walked by our
table, then through the adjacent doorway and sat in one of the
love seats positioned about the room in front of the bar. She was
wearing jeans and a white T-shirt, with a long-sleeve cotton
sweater draped over her shoulders. She was a young woman
with a thin build and she walked with a wonderful lack of
pretense, moving between the tables on the veranda with the
delicate step of a show horse. From our table, I could see her
sitting beneath a ceiling fan and playing with a swizzle stick
she'd found lying on the table in front of her. A waiter came by,
but she waved him off, then shouted something at him in French
as he walked away. He returned, dragging a large, black dog by
one of its front paws. When the dog saw Gabby, it freed its paw

from the waiter's grasp, then padded over to the young woman and placed its chin in one of her hands. She stroked the dog behind an ear for a while, then it curled up at her feet, nudging her hand, every now and then, for another soothing stroke or two.

She was sitting in silence. I wondered what she was doing there without food or drink, or companionship – save for the beast at her feet – just staring blankly into space. Tom's antennae had gone up immediately. I must say she caught your eye, her white skin and ash-blonde hair contrasting the dark corners of the room like a bed sheet flapping in the moonlight. Tom was not much company once he'd seen her. He'd had quite a few bottles of Prestige and was beginning to get loud, but Tom was an engaging man even when he'd had a lot of beer. He had a killer smile and a disarming sense of humor and people forgave him a lot for that. He waited for me to finish a sentence, then got up and started toward the archway.

"Tom," I said, "wait a minute," but he ignored me. I was sure he was going to create some kind of commotion, and the young woman didn't look like she went well with that kind of scene, so I followed him inside.

Gabby seemed, at first, as if she wanted to alert the dog. There was a stern look of annoyance in the set of her jaw, a look that announced we had invaded her territory and she was not about to give up her seat, irrespective of the assault on her space. The downward curve at the corners of her mouth became more pronounced as Tom sat down in a sofa opposite, the look of Gabby's pale, blue eyes darkening just a shade. Although she looked like she knew how to deal with interruptions, I was sure she'd never met anyone like Tom before. I sat alongside him to mediate, keeping a wary eye on the dog, but it seemed dead to the world.

"Come here often?" Tom inquired.

I blurted out a laugh.

She obviously considered the come-on not even worthy of a response and chose to ignore it. Instead, she slipped off her sandals, pulled her legs up under her on the sofa and looked off

in the opposite direction – as if neither of us existed – toward
the bar, where a heavy-set man in white shirt and slacks was
conversing with a young man in a beautifully tailored business
suit. The heavy-set man was gesturing animatedly with a thick
cigar held between two stiffened fingers.

"Let's go back to our table, Tom," I said, watching the girl,
who made not the slightest attempt to acknowledge our
presence. "It's clear the young woman doesn't want to be
disturbed." I put my hand on Tom's arm, but he ignored it and
after a few moments, I withdrew it, awkwardly.

The young woman turned back in our direction. "I'm sure
you have something you want to say to me," she opened, "so
please get to it, then –"

"Nope," Tom cut her off, "not really."

A waiter had approached our tense trio.

"I'd offer to buy you a drink," Tom said, never taking his
eyes from hers, which, likewise, remained locked on his, "but I'm
not sure what the age limit is down here."

"There is none," she said.

"Nonetheless, I'd suggest a virgin colada," he replied. His
face lit into his all-encompassing smile, which could take a
blowtorch to a glacier.

She couldn't hold back the quiver of a smile.

"Barbancourt, neat," she said to the waiter. "Put it on my
tab. These gentlemen will be ordering separately."

I raised my eyebrows, impressed with her choice of the
country's world class rum, never to be polluted by even so much
as an ice cube. Tom added rows of piano teeth to his smile and
ordered two bottles of Prestige for us. He continued to stare at
Gabby as if by doing so he could penetrate the shield she'd
raised between us. "I'm just trying to make conversation," he
said in her direction, "break the ice, so to speak . . . be sociable."

Gabby, however, was back to watching the bar, where the
man in white now began to cast concerned looks our way. He
was shifting his weight from leg to leg, nervously. Finally he
made a wave of his hand to excuse himself and began to drain
his drink.

"The man about to interrupt our little 'conversation' is my stepfather," Gabby said, turning suddenly toward Tom. "He owns pieces of several businesses down here that supply goods for his businesses in New York. The handsome one in the suit is his local banker here. My stepfather owns him, as well."

Gabby's stepfather left the banker and approached.

". . . Yes," Gabby said to Tom, as the man drew near, "I'd be happy to join you at casino, tonight. Let me go change. I'll only be a few minutes."

The man in white watched, disapprovingly, a dark, angry look on his face, as she got up and started in the direction of the staircase near the front desk. Then, almost as an afterthought, she stopped and, turning ever-so-slightly back toward us, said, "gentlemen, this is Harry Gordon, my stepfather."

"Gabrielle," he countered, but she had already turned away, slipped the sweater from both her shoulders, and as a continuation of the same motion, flung it over her left shoulder and started up the stairs, once again setting in motion the wonderfully orchestrated movement of her walk.

Tom smiled. "A pleasure," he said. "I'd love to stay and chat, but I must be off to change as well. It seems I have a date for the casino."

I was astonished by the turn of events. But things like that happened to Tom. For my part, however, I didn't want to mop up with Harry, so I excused myself, as well, and headed for my room to transcribe my thoughts.

He stood at the craps table, making his point, roll after roll, until he feigned boredom and said he had a date with a deck of cards. She had positioned herself at the far end of the table, not needing to see the numbers on the ivories; she a figure in white ivory far more intriguing than the compliant cubes. At the blackjack table, her hand rested upon his shoulder, fingers occasionally feathering his neck. When the one-eyed jack peaked from behind the ace, he swept up his winnings, tossed a chip toward the dealer, and headed for the exit, she gripping his arm, her head nestled against his shoulder . . .

* * * * *

I flew to the north coast, before dawn the next morning, to
interview an archaeologist who had made some important
discoveries concerning the early voyages of Columbus.
Throughout the day, however, my thoughts were often loose in
space, tracking Tom and Gabby and what it must be like to force
an encounter with a beautiful young woman and have it resolve
the way that one had worked out for Tom. I was envious, of
course, jealous really, and anxious for dinner and the chance to
talk with him about it, but he had not answered the messages I'd
left for him all day, was not in his room when I returned to the
hotel, and was not available at dinnertime. I dined without him,
which allowed for my scribbled observations of the play
unfolding about me.

*Katherine, the art dealer from Philadelphia, was chatting with
Magy who was from Paris and designed sweaters, which sold for
hundreds of dollars, but cost only a few dollars to make in Haiti.
Katherine and Magy were always together... At a small table by
the doorway to the veranda, a young woman was trying very hard
to be noticed by everyone but her male companion, who was quite
a bit older. I'd overheard one of the other guests say he was a
lawyer from "down south somewhere. Very influential." His
companion crossed and uncrossed her legs, each time displaying
seductive flashes of hidden recesses... A table of scrabble players
was paying token attention to the game, but seemed quite
engrossed in the pronouncements of a heavy-set man from New
York who was in the import/export business. He held a cigarette
as if it were a pointer, in a right hand heavy with gold bracelets,
while, between puffs, he spoke with the tone of voice of someone
who is an authority on everything. His wife, in an apricot print
dress, sat alongside and looked bored... At another table, a
middle-aged woman, in a tropical dress far too formfitting for her
excess weight, was talking with two homosexual men who spoke
about nothing but the theatre. Six businessmen from Texas were*

talking and talking and talking business . . . Pickins' slim this evening.

I closed my notebook, signed my check and headed back to my room.

When I came down for a nightcap, several hours later, I spotted Tom and Gabby seated at a large round table in a far corner of the veranda. This time they were already dressed for a night on the town and I decided that despite the size of the table they had chosen, they would probably want to be alone. When Tom saw me, however, he waved me over.

"Where the hell have you been?" he asked. "I've been calling your room all day."

"I've been at Cap-Hatién. You knew that. I left *you* messages." I lowered myself into a chair. Gabby was in the midst of one of her snifters of Barbancourt and looked up only to nod as I sat down. "It was really fascinating," I continued. "The guy I interviewed had broken pottery and other artifacts from a farmer's field that he thinks may indicate it is the site of the settlement Columbus founded after he wrecked the Santa Maria on Christmas Eve –"

"Look, we had a hell of a fine night, last night," he interrupted, "and I was thinking you should join us, tonight."

I was surprised at the invitation, given my already established reluctance to carouse around with him and the added wrinkle of the female companion. I looked over at Gabby, but she just sipped at her drink.

"How'd it go at roulette?" I asked, to avoid answering.

"Lost a couple hundred," he answered. "Listen, do you want to go or don't you? Time's a-fleeting. You can play the slots, or just watch."

"I don't know," I said, feeling foolishly irresolute. "I've got a lot of notes to transcribe."

"Transcribe, damnscribe. Look, why don't you get the hell out of that room for a night?" he persisted. "Besides, you meet some real characters out there. Not dusty old archaeologists."

Anger shot through me. I resented his disparaging my work and, now, making me look like some sort of wimp in front of the young woman. I was about to loose some of my bile upon him when Harry Gordon came through the archway, cast an eye about the dining area, then headed straight for us.

"Act two," Tom said, when he saw Harry coming.

The stepfather went directly over to the girl and said, "Gabrielle, it's time for you to go to your room."

I almost laughed at that. Then, I could see from Harry's expression that he wasn't kidding, that he wasn't mincing words and that tonight he wasn't going to be outmaneuvered.

Tom looked up at the older man and was about to tell him where to get off when Gabby, her head bowed, spoke without looking up. "Tom and I are just talking, Daddy," she said, with just a bit of flutter in her voice, like a child who had been caught misbehaving. "I'll just be few minutes more."

"A few minutes more?" Tom echoed, now staring at the top of her downcast head with a perplexed look on his face.

Harry was unmoved. "It's time," he insisted. He was a man of coarse beginnings, I could see that. His demeanor and his diction had been tainted and no matter how he tried to affect an appearance of breeding, he'd been marked for life.

Gabby raised her head, her face had assumed a pouty-mouthed expression that was oddly infantile and, at the same time, incredibly seductive. I could see by the prune-like expression on Tom's face that he was wrestling with the ridiculousness of a young woman, past the age of consent, a woman who had stayed out to the wee smalls with him at the casino the night before, being ordered to her room by an elder. He also must have been trying to deal with the folly of a man his age having to ask an ersatz parent if his stepdaughter could come out and play. The building tension was resolved when Gabby excused herself, got up from her chair and left the table. Harry headed off in the opposite direction, his chin stuck out in front of him almost parallel to the ground, the look on his face in perfect accord with the smug son-of-a-bitch to whom it belonged. A thin line of smoke from his thick cigar, trailed behind him like the tail of a kite.

I just sat there, unable to erase the pouty-mouthed expression she had assumed, which had imprinted itself, indelibly, in some ineradicable corner of my brain. For Tom, as good as the turn of events had been the night before, they had instead turned badly this night. He told me she had related to him over drinks last night that she had been coming to Oloffson's every year, for the pre-Lenten carnival since her stepfather first took her and her mother to Haiti for the festivities when Gabby was sixteen. Harry Gordon had married Gabby's mother when Gabby was thirteen. Harry became a widower three years later, when the family curse of ovarian cancer claimed Gabby's mother at the age of thirty-eight. When Tom asked, only half-heartedly, if I had the energy to hit a few spots with him, I declined, sure that he would take out his frustrations on alcohol and loose women and I wanted no part of either. Instead, I was relieved to return to my room and my work.

I sat scribbling and crossing out for more than an hour, not pleased with anything that was forthcoming. I needed to send my thoughts to some other place. That would require some inspiration, perhaps some assistance. I headed downstairs to the bar. The crowd had thinned out appreciably, so I asked the bartender to pour me a double Barbancourt in a snifter and returned to my room to write.

The artificial light from the courtyard was strained through the fan-shaped pattern of slats above the louvered windows, casting a seersucker shadow across the ceiling. The design held her attention. Now and then, the abstract geometry of the striped light was interrupted by the blurred movement of a bat darting about its roost, under the eaves near one of spires on the roof, just above her window. She lay naked beneath the sheet, motionless except for the tiny oscillations of her right index finger between her lips; silent except for the barely perceptible sucking sounds the

Tom joined me for breakfast the following morning, was
relating how he had grown bored with nightlife the previous
night. I read his words as an unexpressed admission that it was
no longer any fun without his attractive accoutrement. Gabby
and Harry approached the front desk dressed to depart. A
bellhop rolled up, pushing a cart loaded with their luggage.
Gabby surveyed the room, looked briefly in our direction, but
made no sign of recognition. They were soon descending the
stone steps to street level with the bellhop rolling their bags
down a ramp to join them. With our final cups of coffee, Tom

said he was cutting his trip short and heading back to Miami, effectively leaving my remaining days a return to a deep dive of loneliness barely brightened by the dim flickers of my writing.

*   *   *   *   *

I was back the following year. Harry Gordon was there as well, but this time sans Gabby. I introduced myself and could see by his blank expression that he was searching for some sign of recognition. I convinced him that I had met him and Gabby under benign circumstances so he would not connect me to Tom. I told him I was writing articles about Haiti and he immediately offered to buy me a drink. When I accepted, he launched into an endless stream of promotional bullshit about his various retail businesses, talking on and on about "the superb craftsmanship down here," not a word about the dirt poor wages he was paying for it all. After enduring this for a couple of rounds of drinks, I felt secure in inquiring about Gabby. He eyed me suspiciously for a moment, but I'd assumed the blank expression I'd perfected over the years to set at ease those from whom I needed to gather vital information. After a sip of his drink, he told me Gabby had married a businessman, ten years her senior and moved to Boston. He said he saw little of her, even though she was carrying a child. From the tone and context of his words, it was clear that husband and stepfather did not get along. Harry had lost all of his well-practiced smiles when he spoke of Gabby.

My stories on the Haitian carnival sold well, so returning each year to cover the carnival and update the Haiti section to the guidebook became somewhat of a ritual. I saw Harry again the following year, searching him out simply to get my annual fix on Gabby. He told me she'd had a baby boy, but he still had not seen the child. The following year, he informed me that she had gotten a divorce and that her husband had disappeared with another woman, even younger than Gabby. Her ex had left behind their son and attempted no further contact with Gabby or the boy. Harry said Gabby was having no luck getting child support payments. I wanted to ask why he didn't spend some of his wealth on his step-grandson, but again, Harry had no smiles when he spoke of Gabby.

The following year there was no sign of Harry. What little pleasure I could muster during my trip to Haiti once again was reduced to my nocturnal scribblings on the characters I met or had the opportunity to observe at Oloffson's and the fictional lives I assigned to each. By then, I had assumed Gabby had moved far down the road to whatever outcomes life had in store for her.

Then, I saw her that last year at Oloffson's.

I had been in Haiti for a week, writing a number of pieces on archaeology, the cultural scene and the deteriorating political situation. My first night at my regular base camp in Port-au-Prince, I strutted into the bar area at Oloffson's and ordered a scotch and soda, then swung around to survey the room. Many of the regulars had returned, a good number of those who'd been coming here, this time of year, year after year. Then I noticed a tuft of blond hair sticking above the back of a high-backed armchair, facing away from the bar. It sent a shiver through me. I took my drink and wandered, as casually as I could project, around to the front of the chair, where I did my best impression of a restrained double take. She was wearing a white Jersey dress, with a scoop neck and sleeves that extended halfway down her biceps. Her left leg was crossed atop her right knee, resting there with the kind of delicacy that she defined for me. A thin gold chain, hung with a Saint Christopher medal, lay against the whiteness of her clavicle.

"Gabby?" I said trying to project the feeling that we were old friends who had just bumped into each other. "It's been forever. How *are* you?"

I had doubts she would even remember me as one of the many bit-part players in her life. However, she studied me a moment then nodded and asked would I like to sit down. I asked if I could buy her a drink. She nodded. I motioned for the waiter and she ordered a Barbancourt. I took a seat in an armchair alongside and we made meaningless small talk about our lives since last we'd seen each other. The conversation was halting and odd, punctuated with stretches of awkward silence, since we'd hadn't had any real interaction even during the times we'd met years before.

Nonetheless, she seemed to want to talk, irrespective of how little common ground we shared. She told me she had come to Haiti to put some distance between herself and reality, although that had been difficult because her resources had thinned out considerably. She said Harry had died of a coronary just before Christmas the year prior. She'd found out from Harry's daughter by his first marriage, several weeks after the funeral. He'd left her nothing in his will. That she seemed to want to continue the conversation ventured into directionless small talk, most of it about the places she had worked in lower level management positions. When that topic wore thin, we lapsed into another awkward silence. This time it was broken when she asked me if I'd seen Tom. I said not in many months, that we did not see that much of each other anymore. The look of anticipation that had tightened her face when she'd asked the question, dissipated with my answer. I couldn't help staring at her and noticing that she had acquired some signs of aging. She was only in her late twenties and she had traces of lines in her face. She began to twiddle with her cocktail napkin and her body language indicated that she was getting ready to stand up.

"I think you are a beautiful woman, Gabby," I said. It just erupted out of some need I suddenly had to express my unexpressed concern about her having aged. Then I felt very foolish for having said it. I wanted to completely divert the effect of the foolish comment by saying, "and you've got some destructive fascination with a drunken gigolo, years after you should have outgrown him," but I didn't, of course, and that just made what I had said sound out of context and silly. She didn't react. I'm not even sure she was paying attention.

"Do you talk to him?" she asked, almost reflexively, and settling back into our conversation.

"How do you mean?"

She didn't answer, her gaze lowering to the table before her, where now she was threading and unthreading her fingers. Again, one of the awkward silences, then she let loose a sigh. "I should go and check on Robert," she said finally, convinced, I guess, that I had no further useful information.

"Don't you have one of the hotel's sitters?" I asked.

She didn't answer, again adrift in some far-off corner with her thoughts. We simply didn't communicate well. I tried too hard. I have never been comfortable around beautiful women, never comfortable with silence, the two causes of discomfort often occurring simultaneously. I could see she was wrestling with something and she would talk to me about it when she was ready. I could conjure no way of drawing it out. In a last ditch attempt to continue the conversation, I asked her if I could buy her dinner. That seemed to bring her down from the ether. She nodded.

"Let me go check on Robert and tell the sitter I'll be back up after dinner," she said. We rose from our chairs, she headed for the staircase to her room and I sat back down. I took a sip of my drink and returned to my obsessive inventory of the crowd of regulars who were now filling the room.

An old man, who walked with difficulty and smoked like a chimney, ordered a scotch on the rocks in a tall, frosted glass. "Just one shot," he said sternly, and loudly, to the bartender. "No more doubles." He kept looking over his shoulder as if a wife swinging a rolling pin would rush into the room just minutes behind him. The young bartender measured the single shot for the old man, held it up so the old man could see, and poured it into a tall, frosted glass where it got lost in all that ice. He placed the glass, with a flourish, in front of the old bastard . . . The table of scrabble players was there, of course, once again paying token attention to the game and, once again, fully engrossed in the pronouncements of the heavy-set man from New York who was in

The big black dog huffed around the corner from where it had been sleeping behind the bar, raised its head and sniffed the air, as if wondering what had happened to the scent of Gabby. Apparently now devoid of any good reason to stay, the dog padded off and disappeared behind the swinging doors to the kitchen.

Writing about the interplay around the room was less than fulfilling, especially now that Gabby had reentered the drama. I was thinking about Tom the night we'd first met her. At dinner, he'd been so loud and he used a vulgarity at least once each sentence. I was a bit put off and wondered whether the manager might come by and ask us to quiet down. But I loved Tom's joie de vivre and I didn't care.

There was a trio entertaining the diners, that evening, with a young singer who seemed barely past his middle teens. Tom and the boy joked back and forth, then the boy sang a couple of songs Tom had requested. Tom told him his voice was too deep and that he should have been castrated when he was eleven, but the boy didn't understand. Tom made some vulgar gestures to try to demonstrate and it was making me uncomfortable, so I asked the boy to sing "La Vie." He nodded and rejoined the band. They had an acoustic guitar, a conga drum and a pair of maracas which the boy/leader shook part of the time, then feigned singing into one of them as if it were a mic. The boy played the guitar a while, then passed it to one of the other players without missing a beat. When they'd finished a half-dozen songs, Tom gave the leader ten dollars American, an enormous tip, which the boy immediately pocketed. Tom objected to his keeping it for himself until the boy convinced him he really was the leader and would share the tip with the other two musicians at the end of the night. So Tom, in his pidgin French, told the others he'd given the boy twenty dollars, laughed loudly, and was pointing at the boy with his bottle of Prestige and nodding his head. When he sat back down, he saw

Gabby go by and take her seat on the sofa by the bar and his interest in the music was gone.

She returned as I was finishing a second scotch and soda.

The maitre d' ushered us out onto the veranda where he seated Gabby in a high-backed wicker chair parallel to the concrete balustrade along the veranda and showed me to a seat at right angles to her. The same trio was in a far corner playing the same renditions of the same songs I'd been hearing there for years. The leader looked as if he were now into his early twenties and had grown a moustache to make sure people noticed he'd matured. His voice seemed more strained than in the past, his delivery, for the most part, that of someone bored with his work.

On the waiter's recommendation, we each ordered sea bass, which Gabby barely touched using the tines of her fork to pick out fish bones before spearing the tiniest morsels to put in her mouth. I ordered a bottle of Gran Cru French Chablis in deference to our choice of entrées, but she left half of the one glass the waiter had poured for her. Conversation was just awkward fits and starts, although I was getting more brazen with each glass of wine. By the end of the meal, she had repositioned herself facing the balustrade and stared out into the night. She was agitated about something and made no attempt to mask her edginess. She seemed to want me to come after it.

A tiny lizard ran along balustrade, then leapt to an adjacent bougainvillea. I noted Gabby's eyes following it from where she was resting her arm on the stone railing to where the lizard had leapt over my shoulder. We made eye contact for a moment, then she lowered hers. "Does he ever speak of me?" she asked.

I held my answer a moment, while I debated asking, "who?" Suddenly it became clear that she had come to Haiti, this same Lenten time of year, in hopes of meeting Tom. But Tom had stopped coming with me years before and had moved onto other adventures. "Yes," I said for no good reason, "of course."

Again, she made eye contact – again, a glancing blow – then looked down at her plate and played with the black rice she had barely touched.

The bandleader, who was working the tables for tips, had made it as far as ours. As he prepared to go into his sales pitch, I could see that he recognized me. Then his eyes brightened and he asked where my friend was, "the loud one."

"From five years ago?" I replied.

"Yes," he said, "the loud, good-looking one."

"With the fat wallet," I answered back.

He laughed.

I took out two dollars and asked him to play "La Vie."

"Ah, yes," he said, nodding his head, then rejoined the band and took up a guitar.

"La Vie," Gabby sighed, still fooling with the rice in her plate.

"Oh, come on, Gabby," I said. "You're not going to tell me something like your life is already behind you, are you?"

"Huh?" she said, a bit abruptly, as if my aggressive comment had caught her by surprise. Actually, it caught me by surprise. She had raised her eyebrows and wrinkled her lips like an old woman. A gust of wind blew across the veranda and folded a lock of her blond hair across her forehead. It held there for a moment, then fell back into position alongside her left ear. She stared at me, her eyes boring into mine. "You don't know the whole story," she said.

Surprise, I thought. I never know the whole story, unless, of course, I write it myself.

"The whole story?" I said, finally. "Why, Gabby, how mysterious." I guess the sarcastic tone to my voice was driven by the admission that I came here every year to find her and, now that I had, it left me disoriented. I don't know. I do know that she didn't like the sarcasm.

She started to say something, then stopped.

I kept going. "Gabby," I said, "you seem determined to portray yourself as something tragic and it just won't play."

"Please," she said, "don't get literary."

"Hey," I said, "it's what I do."

She smirked, then fell silent again.

Behind her, in the distance, lightning flashed in horizontal bands of white across the sky. I could smell the rain on the wind, which had picked up and was blowing in directly across the veranda. The clean fresh smell of the wet air filled my nostrils. Then the wind was scented with the fruit blossoms of the tropics and then the cores and rinds rotting in the street in front of the hotel.

"He came to my room that night," she said.

"Who?" I asked. "What are you talking about?"

"Harry. The night I met Tom."

"And me."

She looked at me quizzically.

"The night you met Tom and me."

She shook her head momentarily, then went on. "I sat up and asked what he wanted, but he didn't say anything. He just came over to me."

It began to rain. The first big drops making loud strikes against the eave above the veranda and kicking up a musty smell from the concrete steps just beyond our table. She seemed annoyed by the interruption.

"He was very drunk," she continued. "His body was like a dead weight. I thought he had died *that* night." She stopped and looked at me for a moment. Again, she seemed to be waiting for something to sink in behind the glassy eyes I presented.

She sighed. "I got out from under him –" She stopped abruptly.

I guess now I *was* staring at her.

"I thought about going downstairs and sitting on the veranda . . ." Her words trailed off.

"But, instead, you went to Tom's room," I said with an edge.

"Yes." Her voice was flat.

"The bastard," I said. "The lousy bastard." I'd said it loudly, my drunkenness fully taking hold.

The young man from the band stopped singing. He came over and asked if there were something else I wanted the band to play.

I said no.

He asked if I wanted an encore of "La Vie."

I said, "hell no!"

He left us.

The rain had gotten very heavy now. Each gust of wind blew wet across her face and mine, but I didn't care. The candle on our table flickered but did not go out. A waiter came by and asked if we'd like him to move the table. I said no, without so much as a glance in Gabby's direction. When the waiter left, shaking his head, I thought about making a cutting comment, but turned back to Gabby instead. She was playing with a paper napkin, tearing it into shreds.

"You know, it all sounds very terrible, Gabby," I said. "It's enough to drive a young woman to marry a successful businessman, ten years older than her and move to Boston."

"What?" she said. Her eyebrows furrowed and she seemed confused.

"Your husband? Your baby?"

She let out a laugh, shook her head. "Who told you that?"

"About your husband and your son?"

She nodded.

"Why . . . Harry," I replied, "a couple of years ago."

She just snickered.

Oh my God, I thought. Harry, you bastard. You lousy bastard. Then I thought, how bizarre. There was Tom bouncing around from place to place with no direction, a quest with no objective. Harry, the filthy bastard, was dead of a chest-crushing heart attack. Here was poor old me, with my directionless slingshot life. And there was Gabby, the object of all our interests, fucked over by her stepfather and toting around their bastard son. Shit, she *wasn't* above the fray. She could drift about a room with her light-footed gait, cop a pose in a high-back wicker chair, sip a Barbancourt and gaze off into space thinking her beautiful thoughts. But when you got inside, when you stripped away the wrapping, she was as fucked up as the rest of us. More. Damn, I got a perverse satisfaction in knowing that. I let out a laugh and shook my head. "I'm sorry, Gabby," I said. "I guess I *don't* know the whole story. I'm sure it's all very sad, so sad."

"You're being cruel," she said, once again concentrating on shredding the napkin.

"That's because you want me to be cruel to you, Gabby," I said. "Tonight, you want cruel."

Now, she was wadding the napkin shreds into little balls. "You don't have to be cruel," she replied. There was no emotion in her voice. It was part of a setting that had grown so strange. My reaction to the flatness in her demeanor now was that somehow she had managed to get me to reveal who *I* was. This was supposed to be all about her ... but now the story was about me. Somehow, she had managed to expose me as the lead character in my own story and definitely not a sympathetic one. I felt bested, out-plotted. Suddenly, I felt ... angry.

Two women went by us to the stone steps. A waiter held an umbrella over their heads. One woman was holding the other by the arm. They disappeared down the steps.

"What *should* I have done?" Gabby asked.

Shit, this whole exercise was really getting to me. I let out a sigh of exasperation. The alcohol had, earlier, emboldened me, but now I felt the difference in our alcohol levels was advantage Gabby and she was playing me. I watched her a moment longer, rolling the pieces of napkin into little spheres and lining them up like tiny cannonballs on the table in front of her.

"About that night?" I said, finally. "Or about life in general?" The edge in my voice remained.

A blast of rain blew in again, across the veranda, spraying the left side of her face, which glistened yellow in the candlelight. Her hair seemed darker now, wet against her head. She kept her eyes on her fingers, wadding the little napkin balls. Then, she looked up at me. "You don't have to be cruel," she said, yet again. It was maddening the way she kept stabbing me with that same dagger.

She brushed a wet lock across her forehead with those thin, white fingers. Her nails had only chips of polish left on them, but that looked like the default position for her nails now, the way things were supposed to be: Gabby, put together at any point in time like an abstract painting. I shook my head. She lapsed back into silence.

Suddenly, there was some yelling behind me. I turned to see one of the waiters had burst through the double doors from the kitchen, pulling the black dog by one leg and shouting at it in Creole.

Gabby jumped up. "Stop it!" she shouted, rising from her chair. "Arrête ça!"

He ignored her, dragging the dog along the veranda, all the time shouting in Creole, the dog yelping. When they were at the edge of the staircase, the waiter kicked the dog down the steps and out into the rain.

"You bastard!" she shouted, "batard!" But the waiter was already heading back to the kitchen, his back to her, ignoring her shouts.

"Oh, sit down, Gabby," I said. "It's only a dog. He'll be all right."

"I love animals," she said. She looked very angry, standing there stiff as a billboard, gripping the wicker chair as if she wanted to shred it like the napkins. "They shouldn't be treated like that."

"And people?" I asked.

"People should know better," she shot back.

I asked her to sit down again, but she wouldn't. She shouted something in French at the waiter, now standing near a table to present a check. He ignored her, lingering a moment at the table before going back into the kitchen. "An-i-mal!" she shouted.

"I thought you loved animals," I said as she sat back down.

The comment regained her attention. "You're very nasty tonight," she said.

"Hah!" I laughed.

She froze me with those ice-blue eyes. It was the way she'd looked at Tom that first night, before he sat down to talk to her. It stopped me cold.

"You were always with your damn notebook and pen," she said sliding, as if by protest, back down into the chair. "I didn't want to disturb you."

"So you disturbed Tom instead?"

"Your light was on. I knew you were working." There was something aggressive in her eyes now. I felt on the defensive, vulnerable.

"How did you know he wasn't?" I said, trying to stay aggressive.

"I didn't, but I was hopeful."

I shook my head and stared at her.

She stared back at me, the freeze look was back. Clearly, she didn't like me fighting back. Then, she took a deep breath and her face grew more relaxed.

"He helped me," she said.

I shook my head. I had all to do to keep from laughing, but suddenly, I was no longer comfortable with antagonizing her. "I record things," I said.

"What?"

"My pen, my notebook? I record things."

"Why?" she snapped. It was more a show of anger than a question. I had managed to reroute the conversation, once more, from the subject she really wanted to address.

"I always have," I answered, nonetheless.

"What does that do for you?" She was again on offense, pressing me now.

"I write stories. I sell them."

"So you do it for what you can get out of it." She was sounding almost prosecutorial.

"It's how I earn my living. People ply their trades to earn money. And," I added with an affected smile, "I like it. I like what I do."

"It's an invasion of privacy," she said curtly. She was getting back at me. She had a path she could pursue. I guess she needed to do that. But, I had a feeling, now, that I didn't have much to lose here. That made me feel confident.

"Privacy?" I said. "Don't be absurd. People aren't confiding in me. I observe them, draw my own conclusions, change things around until they are where I like them to be. I make them my own."

She was staring at me now like I was some kind of criminal, confessing to my crimes.

"When I'm writing fiction," I added. "When I'm on a journalistic assignment –"

"You make other people's lives your own? Then you lie about what you see? You're using people."

"Don't be naïve, Gabby," I retorted. "Everyone uses other people." Harry, I wanted to add, then Tom. But I decided not to go down those trails.

"Not everyone," she said, emphatically.

I could see she was waiting for me to accuse her of using people, so I didn't. "Most of what I do is me," I said, instead. "It's my interpretation. It's really me getting out what's inside of me."

"Oh that's so egotistical," she snapped. "You're judging people."

"I'm creating characters," I said. For some reason, I liked that answer. I felt I was regaining some measure of control.

She would have none of it. "You're passing judgment," she repeated. "You're saying this man is like this, that woman is like that. And you don't *like* your characters. I can tell by the way you're talking. You like them so little you amplify what you see as their flaws. Then, you wish them ill. You want them to fall. So you make them fall."

"Since when did you become an authority on my work," I answered, struggling for the floor again, but she continued to talk over me.

"And you hardly ever talk to anyone. I've watched you. You're sucking people into your world and having them act the way *you* want them to."

She took a breath.

"Tell me, Gabby," I said, seizing the opening. "Tell me you don't have opinions about the people around this room."

90

She didn't answer right away. Instead she picked up about a half-dozen of the little paper balls and rolled them around in her hand, then spilled them out onto the table. She watched them intently for a few seconds, as if she were a seer reading something in the way they fell. Then, she looked up at me. "Your opinion is immoral," she said. "You put it down on paper. You record your lies. And you do it with some warped sense that you're creating your version of history."

"History?" I answered quizzically. The notion brought a smile to my face. "History? Where the hell did that come from?"

We both fell silent until she said, finally, "look, I've got to go check on Robert."

"Sure." I took a sip of what was left of my wine. It was warm and I could taste the dry chemical flavor of the potassium in the dregs. "You do that."

She left and I was sure that was that. Hell, I didn't need her for entertainment. The show was going on all around me. I took out my recently maligned notebook and began.

The Grand Hotel Oloffson looked down on Rue de la Guerre in Port-au-Prince like a military dictator addressing a crowd. Oloffson's was civilization shielded by its tall palms and hibiscus from the teeming jungle on the other side of its garden wall. Out the gate, black women walked with a whole day's back-breaking labors in the broken wicker baskets balanced upon their heads. They washed their children in the rain-water runoff along the sides of the road. Men chased you down the street trying to guide you somewhere, direct you anywhere, for a few coins. The people drank water from rusty pipes poking from random holes in the stone walls of the city. Out there, dogs were skinny as rats, scrounging for food scraps the people didn't get to first. But, despite its predominantly American clientele, Oloffson's wasn't some kind of America in absentia. The people who came here, the same time each year, came here to escape America, to say and do things here they couldn't do back there. God only knew what that decrepit old man who kept explaining to the bartender how to pour just enough scotch over the ice in his tumbler, what the hell he was doing here . . .

The import/export man was holding court, speaking at length and with great authority about some subject I was sure he didn't know a damn thing about. But they listened to him, his gallery, as if it were gospel. I had a feeling they had to. Even his wife was envious. But, the import/export man's place at the podium had been purchased not earned, attention to him demanded not accorded, and his wife was the reaper of what he sowed, useless in her own right . . . Katherine, the art dealer, was all smiles, the impresario of furniture store art for those who had recently acquired taste. Magy's smiles were more reserved, perhaps 'refined' was a better word. She was the descendant of ancestors who had had the good taste to stay in Europe. Magy was what Katherine aspired to be but could never become, because Katherine had not been born French . . . The gay men were still talking theatre. They were the sexual vogue du jour, insisting on the right to be treated mainstream, while at the same time deploring the ordinary performances on life's stage of the ordinary. They were at their scrabble game tonight with two old ladies who thoroughly enjoyed the repartee . . . The six businessmen from Texas laughed and drank and smoked and talked the numbers. They were big business today, taking it right out of the mouths of tomorrow . . . The old man from Massachusetts looked like death having to answer for the life it had led. And Gabby . . .

Gabby . . . she had given me hope that she was free, that someone like her had to be free. But there she was, a captive of Harry's resources, bought and paid for by him, and chasing after whomever among the Toms of the world wanted to play for a night. Maybe free without a frame of reference was madness. Maybe free didn't have a language. Maybe it was just another kind of loneliness. I thought for a moment about her young son. She'd hardly mentioned him. I wondered what role he was to play . . . Me? I was the kind of person who would always fall for the Gabbys of the world, but would never have the courage to risk

*exposing myself to rejection. Had Harry married her mother just
to get at Gabby? Harry, now he was a pragmatist. Harry was a
businessman's businessman. Harry was? Pure evil. Tom? He was
a doer. He had had her, then had gotten away, scott free.*

She returned. I didn't expect it. I was blindsided. She
rejoined me at the table.
"Well," she said, "what's the verdict?"
"The verdict?"
She swept her hand across the room. "On them. Who are
they all? What is the meaning of all their lives?"
The brief intermission hadn't washed any of the acid from
her tongue. I looked at her and just shook my head.
"Tell me," she asked, as she sat down, "have you ever
written anything about me?"
The question caught me off guard. I suppose I should have
seen it coming at some point, but it was, for me, an unexpected
change in direction.
"No," I answered, feebly.
"Hah!" she blurted. "I don't believe you."
She was right, of course, and she knew it.
I groped for a better answer. "Nothing I'm happy with," I
said, again lamely. Although that *was* the truth. I hated
everything I'd written about her. And I could see, now, by the
quizzical expression on her face, that she felt I could be telling
the truth.
I started to laugh. I don't know why, I just did. Maybe I
wanted to make her angry. Well, I accomplished that. Her look
turned very hard.
"I don't like you," she said.
"Oh, come on, Gabby," I sputtered. "You sound like a child."
"No," she said, "I don't like you – really."
"You're being silly," I said, now regaining my composure.
She got up.
"Oh, sit down," I said. "I'm sorry."
"Good night," she answered. "I'm going back to my room."

"No," I said, now a note of insistence in my voice, actually a touch of panic. "I'm sorry. Please sit down. I'm trying to understand, but there seems so little common ground."

She said nothing but hoisted her purse strap over her shoulder and turned from the table.

"No," I repeated. I stood up and grabbed her arm. "Don't go. Don't go back to your room."

She pulled her arm free and stepped back from me. I reached for her across the table, but she stepped backward another step toward the stone staircase. I stretched to reach her but lost my footing on the wet tiles. My outstretched arm hit her shoulder and she fell backwards onto the stone staircase, sliding on her side down the three steps to the landing, where the staircase forked left and right. I'd fallen across the table, knocked over a coffee cup and shattered the water glass that was in front of me.

"Oh, my God," I said, with the import of what I'd done finally registering on me. I felt like such a fool.

Two waiters ran to her.

I righted myself and went immediately to the edge of the stairs to help, but the waiters assisting her to her feet were in my way.

"Gabby," I said, the word clutching in my throat, then breaking free for another instant, "Gabby." God, I loved the sound of her name.

The waiters were assisting her back up the stairs. I could see now that she'd skinned her left knee and her dress was soaked and mud-stained. Otherwise, she seemed to be all right. She was going to be all right. Like new. Like . . . new.

They led her by me, but she wouldn't look at me. Not even the angry look. She just stared straight ahead. She wasn't saying anything, not making a sound. Not even a whimper of pain.

"Gabby," I said, this time my voice barely above a whisper. I was horrified. Horrified . . .   Wasn't I?

. . . Hell no, he'd done it on purpose. Strike out at the enemy, anyone who disrespected him.

"Gabby," I said, again my voice barely above a whisper. But
the waiters continued to lead her away from me.

I started after them, but one of them turned and came over
to me. "Monsieur," he said, "we think you should go to your
room."

"What?!" I retorted, then I realized I'd said it loudly. Well,
who gives a fuck?

"What?!" he repeated more aggressively.

They'd gotten Gabby to the stairs by the front desk, leading
to the rooms on the second floor. I started in their direction
once again, but the waiter came over again and put a hand on my
shoulder. "Monsieur," he said, but this time he just let stand the
word.

*He turned on the waiter, who had a smile on his face, all teeth, the
smile they'd taught him to use at a time like this. He thought
about hitting the waiter, but that would have been ridiculously
aggressive. The waiter would never strike back. He knew that.*

I stood there for a few minutes and I guess I looked as if I
was going to hit the waiter because the man in the
import/export business came up to me and said, "Sir, don't you
think enough is enough?"

He glared at the intruder.

I started to respond, to tell him to back off. Then I thought
about saying something clever like: "Do you import or export,
you son of a bitch, you can't have it both ways." I looked around
the room . . .

*He saw the others waiting in anticipation to see what he was
going to do next.*

It was so ridiculous the way they all were staring at me, expecting me to do God knows what, to strike out in frustration, secure in the knowledge that the frustration of unfulfilled dreams would always be a part of the life I led. "Why don't you and your friends just . . ." I was searching for a biting rejoinder but the unfinished sentence just hung there.

He continued to glare at the man in the import/export business. "Why don't you and your friends just go to hell," he said. "You can lead the way."

The import/export man stared at me a moment, his eyes probing deep into mine, then his features seemed to drain of any muscular tension. He just shook his head and turned back toward his entourage.

Why don't you all just go to hell . . . I'm sure they'll show you right in." "Why don't you all just . . ."

'It makes for a far more interesting narrative,' I say. She sighs melodramatically. 'It makes for pulp fiction.' she says. 'I deal in reality. Facts, not unsupported interpretation.' She sips her coffee and seems to study me a moment, awaiting some sort of rejoinder. But I respond with a blank expression.

KEY LARGO

"**H**im," I offer, with a sideways head gesture.

"Who?" she asks, then glances to where I'm gesturing. She studies him for a moment. "What about him?"

Across from our breakfast table at the al fresco dining room of Meliá Cariari Hotel, on the outskirts of San José, the capital city of Costa Rica, is a man who looks annoyingly familiar to me.

"I make him very Boston-Brahmin, very white, light brown hair combed across his forehead in a Kennedy." The target of my ersatz analysis is wearing a pale blue polo shirt, nestled around the pot of his belly, over yellow Bermuda shorts, the wide pant legs accenting the contrast of his spindly legs. "I just can't place him."

"So, why bother?" she asks.

"But I know I've seen him before," I respond, ignoring her comment.

It is a gloriously warm morning. The sunshine on my back and shoulders feels like a hot rock massage at one of those Swedish spas. The woman with whom I am sharing breakfast is editor of one of the magazines which publish my articles. She has spent the better part of a decade reducing my rambling writings to simple sentences, some of which the readers of her magazine might actually understand. But when she is captive in a social situation with me, she must suffer the unedited verbal versions of my literary flights of fancy.

"Perhaps on U.S. TV: a talking head, one of the regulars forever interpreting politics on those all-day/all-night political opinion networks. He doesn't attract hot women in his own environment, but resources and available women in this one equal an extended relationship."

His companion is a beautiful mixed-race girl, skin color favoring black forebears. She has a striking face: dark eyes; angular features; full, maroon lips; the sense of near-perfection tempered by a band of acne over her nose and across her cheeks. Her hair is in tight cornrows. Her tight tank top seductively suggests sumptuous cleavage. She is half his age.

"He wears that smug look of having succeeded where others – me – will fail," I go on. "Ply her with food, drink, trinkets, so he can feel he don't got to pay for it. At least not in the age-old, straight-cash transaction."

"Why are you doing this?" she asks.

"Well," I counter, "this *is* Costa Rica and prostitution *is* legal."

"So, why do you care what he's got going on? Whether he avoids the straight-cash transaction to justify not having to pay for it? Why do you need to transform some observed reality into an alternative reality of your own making?"

"It makes for a far more interesting narrative," I say.

She sighs melodramatically. "It makes for pulp fiction." she says. "I deal in reality. Facts, not unsupported interpretation." She sips her coffee and seems to study me a moment, awaiting some sort of rejoinder. But I respond with a blank expression.

"Well," my editor says, finally tiring of the word play. "See you Monday, Michael. Remember, it's a straight travel piece. This country is the perfect destination for those among our readers who love to travel. I need your essay – operative word, 'essay' – right after you get back, so I can begin the painful process of repairing it. And . . . pleeeeze, don't get into too much trouble while you're here."

"Then why bother to waste a weekend?" I reply.

She drains her cup, then lifts out of her chair. "A straight travel article. You follow? 'I went here, I stayed at this hotel, I ate this for dinner. Straight-ahead travel article."

I answer with a wry smile.

"Oh, gawd," she says, her lips curling, a slow head shake. "You need an outlet for all this. Get some underground publisher. Call yourself . . . I don't know . . . 'Anonymous.' Yes. Call yourself, 'Anonymous.'"

I furrow my brow, look at her quizzically.

Again, the head shake, more pronounced this time. "Monday," she says. "Straight travel piece." She turns, then directs her roll-along luggage toward a line of taxis just outside the main entrance of the hotel.

*　*　*　*　*

This is my third trip to Costa Rica, but this time I'm out of synch. I am wrestling the long-established sense that this is a place of needs-abatement, desires fulfilled. But, this time I'm not sure what my needs are, let alone how to satisfy them. I decide I do need to get in the middle of things, however. Let it play. See where it takes me.

I have taken the ground floor, garden suite at Hotel Grano de Oro, a lovely, converted, turn-of-the-century mansion in San José. The room is furnished with a nod to the property's past: beautiful, handcrafted hardwood furniture; a four-poster, wrought-iron bed; antique furnishings, prints and other accents. There are also accessions to the demands of modern travelers: cable TV, fast wi-fi and email connections. My bathroom is a huge, painted-tile affair with a soothing jacuzzi. A French door, in a sitting room off the bedroom, opens onto a vest-pocket tropical garden, where I can relax with a cool drink. Breezes billow the gauzy curtains that pirouette inside along slatted window blinds opening onto still more fragrant gardens. It's intoxicating. I am transported to a Latin America of another time, or into the pages of a novel by García Márquez, a poem by Neruda. What a place to get laid … except that the management has a house rule about inviting the local ladies back to the hotel, strictly enforced.

I need to reacquaint myself with the heart of the city. It's an easy 20-minute walk from the hotel, a journey of run-on sentences, a stream of scenes in a Whitman poem. Sidewalk vendors are selling lottery tickets, boots, belts, baseball caps, knock-off watches, fruits and vegetables, Latino magazines, used books with tattered covers. The air is heavy with the smell of fried fish, of bad fish. Blanched slabs of meat are piled high in a butcher shop. Crusty tubers in odd shapes overflow boxes in a grocery store. There is the glorious smell of ground coffee. Store after store displays cheap shirts, cheap shoes, occasionally some expensive looking jewelry. An elderly couple hobbles along, hand-in-hand; young girls hold schoolbooks to their breasts; little boys tote knapsacks, horse around. A man with a beet-red face is asleep on a ledge outside an office building, people walking by without interest. Further along the ledge, a man with no legs is begging coins. Children in school uniforms are on line at a Pizza Hut, making their joyful noise. Everywhere there are clots of animated conversation.

Within a few blocks of each other, in the heart of San José, are a half-dozen pickup bars in an area nicknamed "Gringo

Gulch." The most famous of these is Key Largo on Calle 7, just south of Avenida 3, across from Parque Morazan. Here prostitutes, part- and full-time, enact an unscripted floorshow. For a display of the human mating-dance, Key Largo never disappoints. Like Grano de Oro, Key Largo is also a converted in-town mansion, but there the similarity ends. While the ultimate nighttime destination in both places is the bedroom, the answers to "with whom" and "what for" are quite different.

I pass Key Largo. In the bright sunlight of late morning there is no visible activity. Shutters in the window facing the avenue are open and I can hear the faint sounds of workmen banging away inside. Men banging away inside. Irony? I continue my journey.

At the Hotel Del Rey, I walk through the casino, almost choke on the cigarette smoke, then into the Blue Marlin Bar. Three fat Americans are seated at the bar, their guts sagging over their belts, their shirtfront seams stretched to the very limits, buttons near bursting. All have goatees. All are sucking on bottles of weak and watery Bud Light, foreswearing the smooth, lovely taste of the local brew: Imperial. It's five to eleven in the morning. The two men on either side of a loud one in the middle are hanging on his every word, noddingly endorsing his every inane comment. I have a feral urge to punch the loud one in the fucking mouth.

Prostitutes are already working the bar. They are a hard-looking lot, heavily made-up, over-dressed in unattractive eveningwear, inappropriate for the late-morning sun. They seem a good match for the patrons at the bar, however, who nonetheless are riveted to a meaningless mid-season baseball game. I can't get past the concept of sloppy seconds in this place.

I take a seat in a far corner of the barroom. A waitress looks up from her smartphone, approaches. I order an Imperial. Her smile shows her appreciation for my selection of the home brew. She heads off to get my beer. I take out my journal and begin to write . . .

The waitress arrives with my beer. The hard-looking hooker at the bar glances in my direction, yawns, then turns back to the trio at the bar. With each swig, I more and more want to punch the loud-talking son-of-a-bitch in his fucking mouth. I gulp down my beer, close my journal and head back out into the blaring sunshine.

I take a seat on a stone bench in Parque Morazan opposite Key Largo. There is a sexual energy here, even in the disruptive light of a bright sun. Two brunettes leave Key Largo, crisscross before me: maybe early twenties, one with a slightly over-ripe ass, shaped to her jeans; the other in black stretch pants measuring a perfect lower half. Both have jet-black eyes. My interest is rejuvenated. The women around here. Again I begin to write . . .

... The two young women, say their good-byes, kiss on the
cheeks and head off in opposite directions.

*　*　*　*　*

After a late-afternoon siesta, I head out of my suite to join
the intimate gathering in the dining room at Grano de Oro. I
whet my appetite with a martini – straight up, twist of lime –
then feast on filet mignon with a filling of gorgonzola cheese,
which oozes out with each cut of the knife. It begs some sort of
metaphorical analysis, but my wet-blanket breakfast
companion/editor is long gone. I go easy on the wine and
forego an after-dinner drink. I have plans. In the pleasant
coolness of the evening, I opt, again, to walk downtown.

Music and loud conversation spill out onto the stone path
toward the entrance to Key Largo. The three bars, on three sides
of the dance floor, are abuzz with activity. This evening, a three-
piece combo – guitar, bass and drums – is playing loud, strident
interpretations of "classic" British and American rock 'n' roll,
including some of the worst covers of The Beatles I've ever
heard. People are not here for the music. Well, maybe a few are.
Two couples are doing interpretative dances to "She Loves You."
Among them, is a skinny, bald-headed man with a hook nose and
watery eyes, paired with one of the more-blatant whores, in
skin-tight, white pants. He is performing a ludicrous shimmy,
trying to stay with her. It looks like the death dance of an aging
wood stork, which simply will not accept the limitations of once-
responsive limbs. I am entranced by his orange sport coat and
his fumbling footwork. What is he thinking? Then I feel a pang
of guilt because I've been known to drink and dance and it ain't
that much prettier. I decide instead of guzzling beers I'll sip a
rum and Coke. Sip. The bar-mistress slides the drink across to
me and I take a seat.

A woman with pale brown skin and a torrent of black hair –
wet, just-out-of-the-shower look – positioned against the
archway that opens onto the dance floor . . . makes eye contact.
She purses her lips briefly. It's more a quiver. There, then gone.
Unexpectedly subtle and, in its ephemeral line, very provocative.
I float a brief smile in her direction, but I feel mine wears
foolishly. She smiles more broadly. I am not sure if she is
mocking me.

I turn away from the dance floor, survey the rest of the
room. A whore wanders in from the street, no doubt fresh from
a rendezvous. She is a girl of maybe 25, with small breasts and
large hips tamped into a sausage casing of a dress, her buttocks
pressed so tightly together she has nullified the crease, the rise
and fall that so enthralls a man. I imagine the explosive release
that comes with unzipping her dress. It is comical.

On the opposite side of the bar, an American, too old for his
long, curly-blond hair, is buying beers for two women in a
heated back-and-forth conversation, he seemingly encouraging a
friendly competition, perhaps a price war . . . perhaps a
threesome. Catty-corner to me, three women are in animated
conversation, alternately sizing up the customer base. One,
whose incongruously ash-blond hair belies her dark skin
coloring, seems the groupings central figure. Her abnormally
round, silicone breasts appear restrained by the elasticized,
upper-body version of her co-workers butt, above the line of a
silky, black dress. When she sees me glance over, she purses her
lips; no subtlety with this one.

I glance back in the direction of the woman on the stool in
the threshold. She does the lip thing again. Despite my nursing
the rum, the smile is having its effect. She is a lascivious Mona
Lisa. I feel the need to get in the game, or at least play for a
while. I flick my eyes in the direction of the toilettes to the right
of the dance floor, gulp down the rest of my drink, rise from my
stool. I note her rise from her stool. Still got it, man.

The blonde-headed whore with the silicone breasts raises
her right leg to impede my progress. She flashes the broad smile
again, seriously gap-toothed; should have spent the money on

dentistry. I stroke the synthetic surface of her hose, then push gently against her leg until it falls away. She raises her leg again, but I slide by. It's a playful gesture, performed to extend the moment of contact, establish a back-up.

My follower joins me in the large anteroom outside the bathrooms. We retreat into a shadowy corner to negotiate.

"Hoondred dollar," she says, bypassing any need to do the exchange-rate math. She runs a velvet hand across the back of my neck, embraces me in the crook of her arm. Sales promotion.

I run my hand down her back and over her buttocks. I can feel no elastic bands beneath her dress. I gaze into her smoky face, note the thin line of a scar, just off the center of her forehead: the mark of some African ritual, the strike of an angry boyfriend, a childhood accident. She has a slim, perfect nose; the high cheekbones of an Amerindian ancestor; the café-con-leche skin coloring of a mestiza . . . but, those pale blue eyes, knifing into mine? Anglo lineage? I am beginning to feel the effects of the rum . . .

. . . emerging from the beautiful, tiled bathroom in my suite, having washed and blotted the smoke-infused sweat from my face. She is standing at the foot of the bed, her back to me. Her dress is draped haphazardly across a valet stand by the armoire. She is in her bra and panties. Her hands are behind her back, fingers at the clasp of the bra. She unhooks it. Her breasts swing free. She wipes the sweat from beneath them with the bra, then tosses it at the valet stand. It catches a corner, hangs a moment, then falls to the floor. She pulls the panties down to her knees, wriggles them to her ankles, removes her left leg, then kicks them toward the valet with her right leg. Not even close. She turns toward me. God . . . Straight travel article? I went here, I stayed at this hotel, I did what? . . .

"Hoondred dollar," the mestiza says, again, still awaiting my reply.

"No tengo," I say, placing my foot on a wrecked barstool shunted away to the dark corner of this tawdry room. Directly the words have passed my lips, I am not comfortable with my lie, where lies are anticipated, expected. I have the money.

"No *es* mucho," she counters, frowning.

"No," I recover, "eez not too much."

She smiles, the wrinkle in her lips just slightly more pronounced.

"Fee-teen minutes," I say, to buy some time, *free* time.

Her smile crumples into a frown. I read it's not my language; it's the delay. She shakes her head and sidles off, back toward her seat between the dance floor and the bar.

I am embarrassed by the interaction. What is this? Since I speak lousy Spanish, I compensate by speaking broken English? Coo-ool.

A man with dense, curly-black hair and a thick black beard emerges from the men's room, struggling with the final inch of his zipper. I watch as he recedes to one of the other bars. I resume my place at the bar, my elbows on the wood surface, my body square to the barmaid, my back to the dance floor. I'm resisting. Impressive.

I feel the knifing blue eyes on me. Or is it my ego taking command, basking now in the anticipation of a major conquest? Scoring with a whore? And that issue isn't even settled, yet. She will no doubt tire of me, my hesitation. I glance at her again. Now she feigns disinterest. The dance continues.

I fold into the dynamic around the bar. It is a less-interesting distraction. The barmaid has taken it upon herself to pour me another Cuba libre, replacing the watered-down glass on the coaster before me, taking a handful of colones from the money I have left on the bar. This time, I swallow half the drink in one gulp. It is mostly libre, or whatever the hell they call rum in Coobre. The bits and pieces of conversation are inane. When first I visited here years ago, eaves-dropping was good sport. "That's miles up the Sarapiquí, in dense jungle." "The boat will be there at midnight?" "Get the two passports and considerate it done."

I sense movement. She has sashayed over, attached herself to me, pressing her sex to my hip. The hard sell. Her body assumes the contours of mine, in a vertical rendition of nocturnal spooning. Her hair smells of ripe cantaloupe.

"Drink?" I ask. She nods, says something indecipherable to the bar-mistress, who takes another handful of colones from my stack, then returns with a glass filled with a cloudy white liquid. My . . . attachment smiles and takes a sip. I try to focus for a moment on my drink glass. Focus. Focus on . . .

. . . the glass sweating on the antique end table. Breezes blowing through the slatted windows billow the sheer drapes, carrying in the extracted scents of the tropical garden, just outside. She is naked above me, framed by the wrought iron of the four-poster bed. The wet-black strands of her hair tease her naked shoulders just above the angular outlines of her clavicle. Her breasts are the perfect curves of a young female, her dark nipples tightened and erect, a northern reaction to the southern connection. Her knees, her lower legs press against my haunches. A corner of the translucent drapes brushes across her face, forming a momentary veil, then falls back to the window. Her bottom rises and falls . . .

The aging, long-curly-headed American has made his selection, but the also-ran is engaging him in an animated conversation. Her victorious colleague rests her cheek on his shoulder, her look distant and disinterested, until the two-for-slightly-more-than-the-price-of-one discussion dissembles the first girl's take for the night and she snaps her head erect. She blurts a curt "no!" at her conniving rival. The man, once again, is reduced to indecision. This threebie thing has him going. Clearly, this will take a while longer to sort out.

My head is floating in a cloud of bar rum. My creative instincts are taking hold, my inhibitions fading with the predicted effects of the alcohol. Suddenly, a chill runs through me. She is the most beautiful woman here. Possibly the most beautiful woman I have ever seen. And, now . . . she is gone?

I turn completely around in my chair and gasp in relief. She is there, once again on her seat in the archway, staring, over her shoulder, in my direction. Her head is cocked forward and turned obliquely toward me. She presents just a bit more curl in her lip. I smile. This time I feel I have gotten it right. She nods. She rises from her stool and heads for the exit. I take a deep breath and drain my glass.

*　*　*　*　*

United Flight from San José to Newark. I am in business class, sipping a Bloody Mary. I remove my journal from my backpack, open it, begin to read:

"Oh, gawd," she says, her lips curling, a slow head shake. "You need an outlet for all this. Get some underground publisher. Call yourself . . . I don't know . . . 'Anonymous.' Yes. Call yourself, 'Anonymous.'"

I furrow my brow, look at her quizzically.

Again, the head shake, more pronounced this time. "Monday," she says. "Straight travel piece." She turns, then directs her roll-along luggage toward a line of taxis just outside the main entrance of the hotel.

I study her retreat.　It's an appropriate descriptive: "retreat." How she walks, rolling that luggage. A kind of slouch. Head slightly bent. Defeated. Retreating into . . . Straight travel piece? That's it? That's all to show for your life as a writer? As an editor? I went here, I stayed at this hotel, I ate this for dinner?

Oh, gawd? Yes! Of course. The manuscripts in the attic, an old file cabinet in the basement. The formulaic rejection letters. Defeat, where once there was promise. "Not what we're looking for at this time." At this time? At any *time? Now, it's how she gets back at the world. At me. Reduce my art to a formulaic travel piece. Reduce me . . . to her. Look at the way she is standing there, waiting for the next taxi in line, her thoughts wrestling with . . .*

࿐

*I asked if she were running for the exercise and she said yes,
but that she'd like to do the New York Marathon someday.*

THE POLICEMAN'S WIFE

"**H**e's police. Some kinda big shot."

Carlo, my gardener, was my information source for
everything: the best house painter, carpenter, electrician, even
the guy who cleaned my fireplace chimney. He was also my best
source of local intelligence, now, on my new next door
neighbors.

"She's retired," he went on.

"Retired?" I questioned. "I've only had a glimpse of her, but
she doesn't look that old."

"Some kinda disability. She was police, too."

"O.K.," I said with a smile, "since you have the complete dossier on the family, who is the young woman in the powder blue Volkswagen Beetle, who comes almost every morning?"

"She comes to help with the boy. He's no good." Sometimes Carlo's English is altered just enough by his Calabrian accent that I'm not quite sure what I've heard.

"No good?" I questioned. "He on drugs or something?"

"Nooo. A policeman's son? He's crippled."

"Crippled?"

"In a wheelchair." Carlo reached down to re-crank his riding mower. "Sad story," he added, then swung the mower through a one-eighty and continued with my lawn.

Hell, they were *my* next-door neighbors and *he* knew about them before I did.

The husband was a stealth neighbor. I'd only seen him for a brief moment as I set off on my run one morning. He came out to hand a manila envelope to someone waiting in a black, late model Ford, with darkened windows and all kinds of antennas sticking out of the roof. We nodded to each other.

During the course of the next several weeks, I saw her outside on sunny days, with her German shepherd, her son in his wheelchair, and the young woman in the Volkswagen who had been hired to help with the boy. The son was clearly, severely disabled, his head bent so low it nearly touched the chair's armrest. When he raised it, it appeared as if he did not have the strength to hold it up for long. Nonetheless, the two women often tried to entertain him by throwing a frisbee about and having the dog retrieve it. But there just didn't appear to be too much they could do for the boy.

Finally, I met her one morning, just before the outset of my morning run. She had gotten out of a black, Lexus SUV and was heading for her front door when she noticed me finishing up my stretches and stopped where her property abutted mine.

"You Michael Rhodes?" she questioned, walking onto and across my lawn to where I was standing.

"Yes," I answered somewhat haltingly, wondering how she knew my name.

"Carlo, the gardener," she said, as if responding to my questioning look. "He said I should meet you. He said that you were a very interesting man." She held out her hand. "I'm Laura Brennan."

I took her hand and nodded. "You should listen to Carlo," I said, smiling. "He's very wise."

She smiled. It was infectious, genuinely warm. "All right then," she replied, letting out a bit of a laugh. "He said you were a writer. *That's* interesting."

"Yes," I answered, "I am a writer. Interesting? I don't know."

"What kind of things do you write?"

Over the years, I've come to dislike the question, for I've been a journeyman writer, scrambling for whatever I could find in the way of work, and the questioner either perceives that right off from my answer or is unduly impressed by the litany of genres where I've been published. My stock answer is: "Anything I can get paid for."

"Like?" She persisted.

"I have a number of newspapers and magazines for which I write features on a regular basis; some websites where I blog. I have a corporate client for whom I do marketing plans and other assorted business stuff, which pays most of the bills. And, like most writers, I am a frustrated novelist."

"Impressive." There was warmth to her tone that seemed to go well with her smile. "Have you written any novels I would be familiar with?" she asked.

"God, no," I replied. "But, hey, I did self-publish one that sold a couple of hundred copies and is now out for a look-see with a Hollywood production company."

"Wow, now that sounds exciting," she said her smile brightening.

"A slim possibility at best that anything will come of it," I said. "But hope springs eternal."

"Don't be such a pessimist," she replied, almost sounding now like a remonstrative parent. "Who knows, that could be your big break."

"Thanks for the sentiment," I said. "Too bad you're not an exec with the movie company. Anyway, thanks, that's sweet of you."

There was a pause, as if we had exhausted all topics of an initial conversation, then, "you run often?" she asked.

"Pretty much every day."

"I used to run," she said, "before my surgery. I want to get back into it."

I hesitated a moment, as if expecting her to add something, but when that was not forthcoming, I said, "Well, this town is a good place for it. There are not a lot of dangerous streets with fast-moving traffic. The high school is about a mile from here and the track there is good if you want to time your pace. I usually do a mile or two on it most mornings."

"That's good to know," she replied. "Gotta take off some pounds and get my cardio back where it belongs."

She was wearing jeans and a polo shirt and, from what I could see, looked to be in decent shape. I wanted to say something to that effect, but I decided that would be a bit forward after just meeting her.

She was one of those attractive women whose good looks lay in their understatement. Her hair was light brown, with lighter highlights, cut to just below the top of her neck, and framing her face in a pleasing oval. She had features that were an attractive array, although nothing dramatic about the shape of her face, the slope of her nose, the fullness of her mouth, but nonetheless defining a face that said pretty, in an American, girl-next-door kind of way. Her smile, however, the flash in her greenish, hazel eyes, conveyed a warmth that made you feel you did want to be at least some part of her universe.

"Here's hoping I see you up there some morning," I said.

"Yes," she answered. Then the conversation just seemed to have exhausted itself. "Well," she said, "gotta go. Nice to meet you, Michael."

"You as well, Laura."

I walked to the edge of the property, then started a slow jog down the road. There is something about her, I thought. You like her as soon as you meet her.

*   *   *   *   *

One of the rooms in my new neighbors' house faced the small window in my master bathroom. The fact that the room in her house lacked shades to cover the large picture window and smaller vertical ones on each side, I did not find unusual, since ordering those kinds of accouterments often took some time. But when months had gone by and still nothing, I assumed they were just going to leave them without shades, perhaps to maximize the light for what appeared to be a living room or family room.

With those windows shade-less, I couldn't help but glance over there each time I used the bathroom and as often as not, I could see Laura moving about the room. There was nothing untoward about my looking across to the window, since my neighbors had opted not to shield the room but it was not as if it were a bathroom or a bedroom, where something intimate might occur. Nonetheless, the fact that I could gain a glimpse of something about Laura's day, and that she was unaware of being observed, began to take on a level of excitement for me. Each time I would use my bathroom, I would glance over to get a brief glimpse of her private life. I could not help feeling how strangely erotic those few frames of her life were becoming for me, despite the fact that all she was doing was puttering about the room.

By late autumn, I'd only seen her outside a few times more, just to wave while she went from her SUV to her front door or vice versa. But, with the coming of winter, life here on Long Island migrated indoors, for the most part. I'd not seen the husband at all since that first brief encounter. Then, one day mid-winter, a twenty-degree, twenty-mile-per-hour-wind morning, the husband came out of the house carrying a manila envelope and walking toward the black Ford parked in front,

113

just as I was about to set off on my run. We made eye contact and it demanded some sort of verbal exchange.

"I'm Michael," I offered, hopping up and down to stay warm, "your next-door neighbor."

"Yes," he answered, "I know."

I continued hopping in place, while he stood there file folder in hand, until, seemingly as an afterthought, he said, "Jim Brennan," and offered his hand, ungloved despite the weather. I removed the glove I was wearing and shook his hand.

"Well," I said, "I need to head off and work up some body heat before I freeze to death."

He nodded, turned from me and began talking to the driver of the car. I headed off down the road.

*   *   *   *   *

Throughout the winter, I'd had brief exchanges with Laura a few times, but nothing beyond, "hello, how you doin'?" before cold had turned to spring, the trees began dressing in tiny chartreuse leaves, bulbs and blossoms began painting the neighborhood in gaudy pinks, reds, yellows and the brightest of whites. Then, there she was one morning up at the high school wearing a pair of black tights and going through a series of stretches by the side of the track.   The tights left little to the imagination and everything I noted of what was revealed looked mighty good.

She had her back to the track as I entered and while my first instinct was to shout a hello, I didn't want to startle her, so I ran past and headed off around the oval. By the time I'd come alongside her again, she had turned, saw me and flashed that beautiful smile.

"Hey, neighbor," she said, "don't you say, 'hello'?"

I slowed to a walk and approached. "I didn't want to startle you."

"Oh Kaaay?" More of the killer smile.

I returned the smile, then "Hello?" I responded meekly.

Her smile grew warmer, ushering in a bit of awkward silence. Then, she said, "run a few laps together?"

"Sh-sure."

We stepped out onto the track and started to jog.

"Be gentle with me," she said, again with the smile. "It's been a while since I've done this . . . with a man."

I turned toward her, but she was facing forward trying, then failing, to restrain a bit of a laugh.

"I'll do my best," was all I could muster.

Thus began almost daily runs together, each time meeting up at the track, despite the fact that we were next-door neighbors. After a few weeks, we graduated from the mile around the track at the high school to running a couple on the streets. Laura grew markedly stronger with each passing week. The conversation was most often just convivial accounts of things going on in our lives, with the occasional coquettish comment by her, and the occasional rejoinder by me, as I became more comfortable in our friendship.

Jim Brennan remained a non-entity, with just a word or two passing between us on the rare morning when I would encounter him at the black Ford in front of his house, while I headed up to the track for the daily run with his wife. Although Laura and I never spoke of why the logistics were such, it just seemed an unwritten rule that we would not meet up in front of our houses.

Although Jim was surely aware that the two of us set out running at about the same time each morning, nothing in his demeanor indicated that he gave a damn. In fact, the more the morning runs revealed to me how gregarious Laura was, the less I understood her relationship with taciturn Jim. On the other hand, as not the greatest practitioner of long-term relationships, I did not consider myself much of an authority on what factors made a relationship work.

Eventually, Laura opened up to me about her surgery. She'd had non-malignant fibroid tumors that caused abnormal bleeding and needed to be removed. Her gynecologist recommended a hysterectomy and, since she and Jim had their hands full with their son and did not want any more children, the operation would not affect their family planning.

"However, it did push me into retirement," she said, one morning as we ran on a macadam path in a section of what had become our course, this portion along a beautiful stretch of Long Island Sound.

"How so?" I questioned. "It doesn't sound like something that would prevent you from ever returning to work."

"It wouldn't have," she answered. "It was simply a matter of my having passed the twenty years on the force that would allow me to retire and both Jim and I decided it would be a good idea if I spent more time tending to our son. While I do have that wonderful girl to help me, Patrick requires a good deal of affection, and it is a joy to watch him smile. Jim had just received his appointment as one of the city's top detective supervisors and that, along with my retirement pay, would serve us nicely."

"That all makes sense to me," I replied.

"Yes," she answered, without elaborating.

We were quiet a while, just our rhythmic breathing counterpointing the morning sounds of birds, the wind rustling the trees and the waves lapping against the rocky coast of the sound.

Then, she said, "but it did have an effect on our . . . relationship."

The comment caught me off guard. I didn't know how to respond. I wasn't sure I would be ready for a discussion of what would make a marriage turn a bit rocky or if she would want to discuss anything about intimacies.

When I didn't reply, "for some reason," she took up, the slightest quaver in her voice, "for some reason, the whole idea of what they'd done to my plumbing . . ." She let the sentence trail off.

"Laura," I offered, but she cut me off.

"I'm sorry, Michael," she said, "I shouldn't have gone there with you. I, I just needed to say   . . . something . . . to someone."

I stopped running. She took a few more steps then stopped as well, but continued to face forward, without turning around. We were both at a loss for words. I took a step toward her. She held her ground, bending forward and putting both hands on her knees. Without turning to look at me, who had taken one more step toward her, she said, "damn, why did I go there?"

I moved to her, placed a hand, gently on her left shoulder and said, "because you know you can talk to me."

She turned her head toward me, and, without taking her hands from her knees or straightening up, she said, "I know. Thank you, Michael."

We were down by an area of the sound, thick with cattails and scrub trees trying to eke out an existence in the briny marshland that lay to the waterside of the macadam path.

"Come on," I said, aiding her back to an upright position. "We both need to head back."

She rose to a standing position and said, "Why? Why do we have to head back?" There was an unfamiliar edge to her voice. "Do you have something urgent to attend to? I know I don't."

I let out a long sigh. "Don't you need to get back?" I asked.

"Of course I do," she answered, the edge still there. Then, she let out a sigh of her own and started running again.

I fell in alongside, but shortly we were beside a narrow dirt trail that led into the wooded area of the marsh and suddenly she was heading off down the trail. I followed behind her and when we were out of sight of other runners or bicyclists, who were on the macadam path, she stopped. Bent down again, hands on knees and just stood there in that position, silently again, the only sound that of her breathing.

I walked up to her and stood waiting for her to say something, but she just held the position.

Finally, I said, "Laura, tell me, what do you want me to say? What do you want me to do?"

I was suddenly overwhelmed with intense feelings I had harbored for her from that moment I'd first seen her outside her home, to those moments I'd glimpsed her puttering about behind that un-shaded window to . . . our present circumstance.

She rose to a standing position, but still head down, the posture of someone beaten or carrying a heavy load. Slowly, she lifted her head and stared into my eyes. It was a look of intense affection. Then she said, "Could you hold me, Michael?"

We were on a trail not far from where the brightening morning was attracting more and more runners, bicyclists, skateboarders, whatever. I was with the wife of an important police captain and . . . I didn't give a damn about my surroundings or how anything we'd do would appear to the outside world. I pulled her gently to my chest and held her, feeling the warmth of what we had generated during our run, but also a warmth that had nothing to do with exercise. She lay her head on my shoulder and ran an arm around my neck, an embrace I felt I could hold forever. Then she raised her head, looked into my eyes for a moment and, instinctively, we kissed. The taste of her mouth, the scent of her body were beyond lovely. The moment was fraught with that realization two people have that something about their togetherness is special. What else to do at this point was uncharted territory.

We disengaged and she said, "come," first taking my hand, then letting it drop, "we need to get going."

"Yes," I answered and we were off and running again.

*　*　*　*　*

For the next three days, Laura did not come out for the morning runs and I, of course, did not know what to think, except that her absence was not a good sign. There was no way I could get in touch with her that I was comfortable with, certainly not phoning or going to her front door. All manner of scenarios were running through my mind, none of them positive. Had she used our moment of intimacy to confront her husband about his lack of intimacy? Had she felt so guilty, she confessed to him in a tearful mea culpa? Had someone who knew Jim Brennan spotted us? Along with beating myself up for helping to create this situation with her, I also played out defenses for my actions. *She* had been the aggressor. I had been caught completely off guard. I was a divorcee; she a married woman. For Christ's sake, we had only kissed, briefly, then went back to our lives.

None of these thoughts had me feeling good about myself, when, mid-morning of the fourth day, she called. "Michael," she said, "we need to talk."

"Of course," I answered, but before the conversation went any further, she said, "can you take a walk up to the high school? I'll drive up about 20 minutes after you start out and pick you up. Then we can go somewhere and talk."

"I'll leave in five minutes," I said.

"See you in a little while," she answered and hung up.

I finished a sentence in an article I was typing, closed out of the computer program, made a bathroom stop and headed out. My thoughts, while I walked toward the high school, were filled with many of the scenarios I'd been analyzing during the previous three days, still nothing more in the way of good answers. As I turned onto the road that ran along one side of the running track, I could hear a car approaching, turned and recognized her black Lexus SUV. She pulled up to me, slowed to a stop and I got in.

"Thank you, Michael, for doing this," she said and drove off.

"It's O.K.," I answered and waited for her to lead the conversation.

"I know a spot," she said, "where we can talk."

Not far from the high school was a nature preserve, with a mansion, formerly owned by a ridiculously wealthy, early twentieth century robber baron, the building now the headquarters for the park staff. A road led from the preserve's entrance to the mansion, around the front of the building, then out an exit and back onto the main road. The property had a number of walking trails, used mostly by bird-watchers and other assorted nature-lovers. It also had a little-used road that led down to a dilapidated building where four garages once must have held some of those vintage Jazz Age Rolls Royces or Cadillacs, with chauffeurs keeping them in gleaming condition. Laura pulled the SUV off the road, onto a weedy lawn, then behind the beat-up building, pretty much sheltering us, even in the unlikely event that someone might decide to drive down the road. She shut down the engine and turned toward me.

"I'm sure you feel as I do," she began, "that we needed to talk."

"Yes," I answered, "I'm so sorry – "

"You're sorry?" she cut me off, a perplexed expression on her face. "For what?"

"Clearly," I said, "I've caused you anguish."

"You caused me anguish?"

"Laura," I said, "we haven't spoken since . . . since . . . I've had a bad feeling about this. I was sure I hurt you."

"Michael," she replied, shaking her head. "Oh, Mike, Mike, Mike. O.K., yes, you have caused me anguish, but if you think it has anything to do with guilty feelings, you could not be more mistaken."

"Well," I said, "here I am again, not sure what to say."

"I was struggling, yes," she said. "I was struggling with how *good* it felt."

She flashed that deadly smile of hers, then she fell silent, again staring into my eyes, as she had done when that look had instigated our kiss. Again, I felt the warmth her look generated. She reached toward me and placed a hand on my cheek, then shook her head.

"Oh, Michael –"

I kissed her.

Suddenly, she lifted herself over the console, to my side of the SUV, and into my lap. We were locked in an embrace, kissing repeatedly; the taste of her mouth, the smooth silk of her face, the smell of her hair, all of it taking control of my actions: my arms about her, then running a hand over her cheek; kissing her cheek, her forehead, her mouth . . . the glorious taste of her mouth.

She pulled away from me and let her head fall against the headrest. She let out a deep breath, then just stared at the roof of the SUV, a contemplative look on her face, as if she would sort this all out.

"You're taking me to a place I've never been," I said, finally. "What do I do with this?"

She smiled. "You know, Michael," she said, turning her head toward me, a slight smirk on her face, as if I had broken her concentration, "for a writer, you say all the wrong things."

"I –"

She was back to kissing me again. Then she took my hand and slid it inside her blouse and onto one of her breasts.

I looked into her eyes, deep into those eyes that had given me such pleasure when they lit into a smile, but it was not a smile that I was seeing now. It was . . . not a smile.

She said nothing but just stroked my hand over her breast.

"You've got to have known how much I've wanted to connect with you," I said in a tone that was approaching a gasp. "What are you doing to me?"

"I don't know, Michael," she whispered. "I don't know."

We were silent for a while. Then she asked, "do you want to leave?"

Now it was I who sent penetrating looks into her eyes. "Of course not," I said. "But . . ." I looked at her a moment, silently, then, "I am completely at sea here, Laura," I said.

"You don't feel anything for me?"

"Of course, I do. You've got to know that."

We sat in silence another moment, then, "Can we move into the back seat?" she asked.

I studied her face, yet again, and let out a breath I'd felt I'd been holding forever. "You know that will change everything," I said. "There'll be no going back."

She sat for a moment, then climbed back over the console, opened the driver's side door, got out, opened the back door and climbed into the rear seat. I just sat there, staring ahead.

"You coming?" she asked.

"I'm trying to keep from getting aroused," I answered, "but it's not working."

As I got out to join her back there, I couldn't help but feel we were like a couple of teenagers who had to sneak off in the family car because we couldn't do this in our bedrooms at our parents' houses.

Everything I could possibly fantasize about being with a woman like her became reality in the back seat of that SUV. The moment she unbuttoned her blouse and exposed the light amber skin tone of her chest to the soft afternoon sunlight. The moment she took off her bra, and I got an unobstructed view of her beautiful breasts. When she opened her jeans, pushed them down to her ankles and slid her left leg out. When she guided my hand beneath the waistband into her panties and I began stroking her sex through the soft, warm hair that surrounded it. Throughout all the foreplay, the taste, the smell of her was intoxicating. When I rolled over and got into position above her, she guided me inside. I'd been in this position, with other women, many times before, but nothing approached the intensity I began to feel with Laura. It was a full body experience, as if electricity ran along the entire surface of my being and out any of the places where my skin contacted hers.

We were holding each other in the tightest of embraces, when I could feel the climax coming. "Kiss me," I said. She pushed her lips firmly against mine. Our bodies jarred in simultaneous spasms. It was one of those moments when mere seconds bear no relationship to any measurements of time. As the spasms dissipated, I felt drained of all energy; my knees, my elbows barely able to support me. When my limbs stopped quivering and I could breathe again, when my eyes could see clearly again, I focused on her face, mere inches from mine. She was wearing a look of consternation, which turned slowly to one of almost beatific affection.

As we separated, and I rolled onto my back, I was stunned by what I had just experienced. Yes, I had done this many times before. No, I had never had such a complete connection with a woman. We had, for a brief few moments, become one person. There was almost nothing that could be said, at this point.

Finally, "that was beautiful," she said.

I nodded, "yes, beautiful," was all I could muster.

We lay in each other's arms, for a few moments, then I said, "I don't think it's wise to be exposed like this, even in a spot this secluded."

"Yes," she sighed and lifted out of my arms. As she pulled up her panties and jeans, "you know," she said, "I'm going to have to put these panties in an old brown paper bag and push them to the bottom of our garbage pail."

I smiled and replied, "or you could just give them to me."

"To do what with?"

"None of your business."

We both laughed as we got dressed quickly and resumed our positions in the front seats.

On our way back to the high school, where she would drop me off for my return walk home, we said little, and I was frightened that she would suffer a post-coital letdown, as she crept back into a day that would be anything but normal.

As we slowed to a stop by the high school, she said, without looking in my direction, "I so want to kiss you once more, Michael, but obviously that would not be a good idea here."

I turned toward her and said, "It kills me not to, but, of course you're right."

"When you step out, leave quickly," she said. "No more conversation."

"Understood."

"Michael," she said, "see you tomorrow for our run?"

I smiled, opened the door and stepped out. She drove off down the road.

*　*　*　*　*

The caller ID said "Brennan."

Why was she calling? Was this wise? Was she having serious recriminations?

I answered the phone.

"Mike," the voice was male. "Jim Brennan."

Instantly, I was petrified to hear his voice, his name.

"Jim . . . How are you?"

123

"Listen, Mike," he replied, "what's this business about the marathon?"

"The marathon?"

"My wife says she's running the marathon. That she is training with you."

I could all but restrain sucking in enough air to hyperventilate. The marathon? Where was she going with this?

"Training with me?" I said, while trying not to sound tentative. Obviously, she had said something to him about our running and it caused some kind of issue. "We run together some mornings when I see her up at the high school track," I went on. "I asked if she were running for exercise and she said yes, but that she also would like to do the New York Marathon some day. I told her I'd done it a few years ago and could offer her some advice based on my experience."

"What kind of advice?" The tone of his voice was repressed anger, measured in the nature of a man accustomed to maintaining control, of himself, and of the situation.

"You work toward the goal slowly," I said, "in a deliberate way, so you don't hurt yourself."

"Could she get hurt?" His curt questions seemed to come before the sound of my answers had even dissipated.

"It takes months to prepare," I said, now regaining a bit of grounding. I was, after all, on a subject I knew well and he appeared to know very little about. "If you try to push it, you can get shin splints that turn into stress fractures, tear a meniscus in your knee, that kind of thing. You have to take a careful, measured approach."

"Why would she want to do that?"

"Run the marathon?" I questioned.

"Yes," he said. "Why would she want to put herself through that?"

"I can't answer for her," I replied. "You'd have to ask your wife. I can only tell you, from my experience, completing that race gives you a great feeling of self-esteem, a real sense of accomplishment. But you have to commit to the training that prepares you to go the distance."

124

"I don't know," he said, "sounds crazy to me."

"Perhaps," I replied. His words, his tone of voice had started to piss me off. "You do need to be a little crazy to take on this challenge," I went on, the slightest touch of sarcasm in my voice.

"Well," he said, "I don't want her to get hurt. We have Patrick to think about and she won't be much help if she's hobbling around on crutches. Can you tell me what you teach will keep her from hurting herself?"

"How can I do that?" I replied. "If she listens to what I suggest, she should be all right. Can I guarantee she won't get hurt . . . How could I do that?"

"I don't know," he said. "Sounds nuts to me."

He rang off abruptly, as if I had simply reinforced what he felt about the whole thing. Great to have that kind of spousal support, I thought.

* * * * *

"I would have preferred you giving me some warning," I said, the following morning, as we finished two laps on the track and headed out onto our course.

"I didn't want you to stress over him calling," she said, as I almost detected a smile.

"Well, I would have stressed," I answered. "You're right about that."

"And, I didn't want you to sound rehearsed," she said.

"Well, no time for that, now, was there?"

"You did great." Damn it, she *was* smiling. I still didn't grasp the humor.

"How do you know that?" I asked, trying to adopt a strained tone.

"He's accepted me running the marathon," she said, "even though he thinks it's crazy."

"Yeah, and what about that?" I asked. "You mention, once to me, that you would one day like to run New York and now we're training for it?"

"Well, think about that," she said. "It gives us a reason to spend time together."

She turned toward me and flashed an exaggerated, toothy smile.

I shook my head, couldn't hold back a laugh. "You know," I said, "you're really good at this. It's starting to get me wondering."

"Wondering?"

"Yes," I continued, "how did you get so good at this?"

Now she was shaking her head. "I used to be a cop," she answered. "I saw all the ways other people screwed up and I made mental notes."

"Why would you do that?"

"Well, more often than not, someone got hurt badly, sometimes killed. And in almost all the cases it was the woman. I didn't want that to happen to me."

"Why would you think you would need to do that?"

"Nothing concrete," she said. "It's an investigative thing. You can't help but analyze where people screw up."

I felt I really needed to know why it appeared she'd been planning something like us for some time, but I was sure persisting would not turn out well.

She began to sense that my concern was real. "I don't know, Michael," she said. "It's what someone with an investigative mindset does. I didn't plan on anything concrete that would involve me, but . . ."

"But . . ."

She seemed at a loss for words. "But here we are and while I never really anticipated meeting someone like you, let alone living next door to someone like you . . . well, there it is. And . . . here I am."

We ran along in silence for a while, then I said, "well the good news is, your running has been getting stronger for several months now, so we are a good way toward where we need to be, but now we need to get serious."

She smiled, broadly, and we headed off toward the cattail marsh.

             *   *   *   *   *

Thus began many months of an ever-intensifying
relationship. Laura was very adept about finding excuses, places
and times for us to continue our affair, whether it was hot sheets
motels or the back seat of the SUV down some secluded road.
She was right about running providing us a natural excuse to
spend time together and she emphasized to her husband that
she would need to work her way up to longer and longer
training runs. A positive byproduct of our relationship was that
she got very strong as a distance runner. When we applied for
the marathon, we both managed to draw places in the lottery.
    She told me her husband worked out of their home one day
each month, the day before the black Ford showed up, because
he had to prepare a report for New York headquarters and he
needed the time and isolation to work it up on his home
computer. The rest of the days, he left early each morning and
spent long hours at his office in the city, which provided us with
much time for longer and longer runs, and longer and longer
assignations. All of our runs took place during the week, when
Laura had the benefit of her helper to look after Patrick.
Weekends, when she and Jim did all the household things they
couldn't do during the week, Laura and I were virtually
incommunicado.
    As the race date approached, I informed her that we would
need to do one very long run. All the training guides suggested,
a month before the race, contestants do a twenty-mile run over
varied terrain, which, unless you suffered an injury, would
pretty much assure you could go the twenty-six mile distance of
the marathon.
    "Let's do it in Central Park on a Saturday," she said.
    "A weekend, in Manhattan," I countered, "I'm confused."
    "I would not want to go anywhere near the city during the
week," she answered, "but on a Saturday, Jim would be stuck
watching Patrick and we would have hours together."

Of course I said yes and, true to form, Laura found us a short stay hotel, midtown on Tenth Avenue, where we celebrated the relative ease with which both of us had done three times around the park.

When we did our last training run three days before the race, she said she was hoping we could celebrate finishing, with a couple of hours at the hotel on Tenth Avenue. With that as an incentive, it was difficult to keep me from trying to run the race at a pace that would seriously jeopardize my finishing. Laura, on the other hand, kept reining me back to the pace that served us well throughout our training.

The marathon was truly one of the high points of my life, watching the joy on her face as we ran across the Verrazano Bridge, all two miles of it undulating, as if the bridge would fly apart under all those pounding feet. We ran for miles up Fourth Avenue in Brooklyn, at one point past a full-blown Latin band. At the halfway point, just over the Kosciusko Bridge from Brooklyn into Queens, we were met by Laura's family: her young helper all smiles; her son, Patrick, lifting his head to see his mother running toward him and smiling broadly, as she stopped for a moment and caressed his cheek with her hand; only Jim, the look of disbelief on his face, making me want to slug him. How could he possibly be so self-absorbed, so unfamiliar with who his wife was, what she was capable of accomplishing, that he seemed clearly surprised she'd made it this far? It grated on me for the next couple of miles until we got to those loud, cheering throngs on Third Avenue in Manhattan.

As we turned off Central Park South for the final three-hundred-eighty-five yards in the park to the finish line at Tavern on the Green, I stopped with about a hundred yards remaining, the finish in sight, and clapped for her as she completed the rest of the course. When I jogged up to the finish line, we fell into each other's arms, sweat painting our bodies, the beautiful scent of hers nothing short of a glory for me.

The flimsy metallic capes the attendants draped over us, the medals they hung around our necks, seemed like the vestments of royalty. The bottle of cold mineral water we each received might as well have been the finest champagne. We walked along some of the nearby footpaths to wind down, then retrieved the duffle bags with our street clothes, pulled on sweatpants and light jackets and headed downtown, using our marathon numbers to enter the subway. As the train motored toward what was rapidly becoming our favorite hotel, her smiles of celebration had oddly dissipated and, when I questioned that, she said she was pretty exhausted.

Ensconced at the hotel, post of making love, she still seemed not in the celebratory moment I was sure completing the race would bring for her. I tried to understand this altered state as a result of what she had said was her post-race exhaustion. We had, after all, just run more than twenty-six miles. But . . .

"You all right?" I asked.

"Yes," she said, without conviction. "Why?"

"Laura," I said, "forgive me. I think I can say I know you intimately, by now. There's something you're not telling me, or are having trouble getting out there."

She seemed in a trance and, again, I've understood what the race could take out of a person, so I lay there for a while, and held my peace.

Finally, without shifting her position, on her back staring up at the ceiling, she said, "Jim's been offered a new position."

I lifted up onto my left elbow and looked at her. She just continued to stare at the ceiling. I pushed a pillow back against the headboard, rose up and sat with my back against it.

"Really?" I questioned.

"Chief of detectives," she answered.

I'd asked a one-word question. I got a three-word answer. I was not getting a good vibe here.

"Sounds impressive," I said.

She didn't reply, continued to avoid eye contact.

Finally, "what is it?" I questioned.

"Chief of detectives . . . in Chicago."

"Chicago?"

"Yes."

As the impact of what she had just revealed fully took hold, I just stared at her, no appropriate words coming to mind.

Finally, she raised the pillow she had been lying upon and pushed it up to her side of the headboard, sat with her back to it, but maintained a clear separation between us. "He heads out there the end of the month," she said. "Patrick and I stay around until we can sell the house."

I just shook my head. "I don't know what to say."

"Well," she replied, finally turning in my direction, "say something."

"I don't want you to leave?"

"Couldn't you say that with conviction?"

"My God, of course, you must know I don't want you to leave. I love you."

"Wow, there's a word I haven't heard before."

I lowered my gaze and shook my head. "What did you want me to say, Laura? You are a married woman. I just didn't feel it was appropriate. But I was sure you knew how I felt."

"I guess."

I looked at her, my eyes filling with sadness. "That hurts," I said. "That . . . hurts."

"I'm sorry," she answered. "I don't mean to hurt you. It's just that my world . . . my world is coming apart . . ."

The sentence just hung there. She looked at me and smiled, not the smile I had come to cherish, but a sardonic one.

"My world is coming apart and I'm a prisoner in it," she said, finally, her eyes taking on a deep sadness.

The thoughts that raced through my head were all self-pitying, all about what *I* would be losing. Was this all about her having an affair before she had to go back to her unhappy life? That beautiful warm smile painted across the face of her sad, sad life. I couldn't help but articulate what I felt. "So, you just wanted a fling before you went back to your life?" I knew the words were a mistake as soon as they passed my lips.

"How dare you?" she said. She stared at me, a tear running down from her left eye.

I studied her a while, "I know you're hurting –"

"Hurting?" she replied, now a distinct edge to her voice. "I'm trapped, God damn it!" Then, "I'm trapped," she repeated, her voice softening and she began to sob softly.

I couldn't bear to see her cry. I wanted to fold her into my arms and somehow plot, with her, the rest of our lives together, but she just stared off toward the blank wall on the opposite side of this cheesy room in this cheesy hotel.

Many times, when I could not help but go over and over that first time with her, I wondered whether there was something primitively appropriate about it, something so devoid of any embellishment it gave the experience its unique purity, a moment that I could never recreate no matter how long I lived. But, the special nature of that moment had faded into our history. We were now simply two people who had come back into a world of other plotlines.

"You knew all along it would end this way, didn't you?" I said. "It would end this way whether there was a Chicago or not. You knew that one day you would have to go back to your life and I would be left to deal with the emptiness it would leave for me."

"Where is this coming from?" she replied. She just stared at me, as if she were trying to understand someone totally unfamiliar to her.

Finally, "Leave him," I said.

She continued to stare at me in silence for a moment, "then what?"

"Come live with me."

She shook her head, said nothing for a moment, then "And Patrick? What about Patrick?"

I was unprepared to answer that. I should have seen it coming, but did not. It just added to my sense of being so unprepared for this, I just didn't have either good questions or good answers for any words that now passed between us.

"You have no answer," she said, "so that *is* your answer."

She was right. I didn't have an answer, at least not the noble one.

"So I guess I was just a fling for you," she said, her tone almost mocking my initial comment about her. "You wanted the benefits of a relationship, but not the responsibilities. At least not the big one that is Patrick."

I still couldn't find anything to say.

She stopped sobbing. Her look softened into a combination of deep sorrow and the affection I had come to love. "Let's just say you gave me a year of joy, Michael, and leave it at that," she said. "Can't you see what you did for me? I love you, Michael, but I'm trapped."

I felt I had nothing more to add. I'd already said I loved her, but even that could not alter the circumstance in which she found herself.

She sat for a while staring at her hands, weaving the fingers into and out of various formations. Then, she looked at me, an almost religious calm settling across her face. "Everything in life is finite," she said. "Can't we just accept what we did as simply the love we got to share for our moment in time? How special that moment in time was for us?"

I didn't answer for a while, then, "yes," I said, without conviction.

We sat in silence, a few more moments, then she said, "we need to go."

I nodded and we both got up and dressed. We said not a word on the train ride all the way home to Long Island.

* * * * *

With the powers that be in Chicago guaranteeing the price of the Brennans' house, it sold quickly. I watched with unfathomable sadness the day the moving van came. An hour after the big truck had left, my doorbell rang and she was standing there.

"Michael, before I leave, I have to tell you, again, that I love you. I've loved you more than anything I could ever imagine."

"And that's supposed to make me feel better?"

"You have given me the great joy of my life, Michael. Thank you."

132

There was a Zen-like calmness to her demeanor. She seemed to have made her peace with what we had meant to each other and she would now take that with her into the remainder of her life. I couldn't help but be impressed with how she was holding it all together. But then, tears began running down her face. I held open my arms and she fell into them.

"You know I love you, Laura," I said, as she began to sob openly.

We remained, locked in that embrace for a few minutes, then she said, "I have to go." She let herself loose, turned and left.

I closed the front door, then stood staring at the back of it for one of those emotional eternities that are, in actuality, just a few moments, but an eternity in terms of their penetrating effects. I reflected on how we had enjoyed, for a brief period, a love most people would never know in a lifetime. But now, with it finished, that just made how special it was so much more difficult to bear. Finally, I turned, walked into my living room, sat on the sofa and cried like I had not cried since I was a small boy.

*　*　*　*　*

For the first several months after Laura's departure, I could barely find reasons to leave the house: the groceries depleting, the dry cleaning piling up, sometimes even the mail sitting in the box by the curb for a day or two, until my carrier removed it and brought it to my door. Then, finally realizing I needed to at least try to move on with my life, I connected online with a woman I had dated for several years in college. She was also a divorcee and had bounced around a few relationships with strangers, which had gone nowhere. When we met for a cup of coffee in Manhattan, near where she owned an apartment, we began to recall those cultural connections we had in common when we dated. We settled into an accommodating friendship. I stayed over in the city when we would go to the theatre, opera, a jazz club or cabaret. She would come to the island to escape the summer heat in the city.

Having had many, many days to reflect upon my year with Laura, the individual elements, the special moments of our time together, I finally had to accept that she was right, of course. However limited, our time was not about any finite number of days together, any effort to extend that time period. Even if we had remained lovers for years, there would never be any way to go beyond that year-long love affair, there would be nothing else that could approach it. I could never even entertain the thought of duplicating that experience with another woman.

Nonetheless, I did have to deal with my human frailties and there were agonizing periods when I missed Laura terribly. But having not heard from her in more than a year, and not really expecting to, ever again, I felt I had finally gotten to the point where I needed to bring that whole episode in my life to closure and accept my return to the prosaic experiences of my former life, the remainder of my life. I sat down at my computer, and began to type:

"He's police. Some kinda big shot."

Carlo, my gardener, was my information source for everything: the best house painter, carpenter, electrician, even the guy who cleaned my fireplace chimney. He was also my best source of local intelligence, now, on my new next door neighbors.

"She's retired," he went on . . .

ᝈ

AT SEA

My romantic interlude with Mrs. . . .

Two-thirty in the a.m. I love reading the time on the Longines. I feel like I do it every few minutes just to look at the watch. Handsome watch. Only the time and a tiny window for the day of the month. Love the minimalism. Two grand, not so minimal. In the jewelry boutique on the Promenade Deck. Duty free.

Powerful light out there. Searching in a sweeping circular motion, as if scanning the seas for U-boats or the sky for the Luftwaffe, enemies long confined to history. Tonight, it's only disrupting the ruler-straight line of the horizon. A tanker or cargo vessel. No lights strung across the decks, ala the lacy look of this, the Royal Princess, one of the court ladies in Royal Cruise Lines fleet of a dozen ships. It's the end of the first full day of an Atlantic crossing. The fog earlier in the day has evaporated exposing a starlit night. Luscious, lightly salted sea air wisps across my face and insinuates into my nostrils. I love the serenity here on the veranda outside the crew quarters. "Restricted Area." No groups of passengers jockeying for space, whenever there is something to see, although the gawkers have thinned to just a straggler here and there, since we departed Brooklyn and sailed beneath the Verrazano Bridge through Lower New York Bay and out into the Atlantic, bound for Southampton in the UK. Already, I can see that I will love the solitude on this veranda. The night shift crews are out of their quarters and on duty; day shift's asleep. Just me, alone in my thoughts.

I've just spent my first night as a dance host on the Princess for an article I'm writing to service travel sections in two dozen newspapers, for which I've self-syndicated my work. Having done many cruises, I've always wondered what it would be like to serve as one of these affectedly debonair dance hosts, whose job it is to fill in for absent husbands, among the mostly elderly women who love cruising, once with, and now without, their significant others, dead or otherwise departed. Since I've always been a decent ballroom dancer, I felt I might be able to pull off this hosting gig, with the imprimatur of a cruise line looking for the publicity.

"I could run through all the possibilities you are likely to encounter with the ladies," explained G. Andrew Cross, the social director, as part of my crash course in becoming a dance host. "But if you've been on all the cruises you claim and seen the dance hosts in action, I'm sure you could draw up that list on your own. This time, however, as opposed to simply being a passenger, when you find yourself looking for a place to run or a corner in which to hide, you are required to play nice and make the ladies feel special. Extra special."

Predictably, I could have used some of those dark corners with my dance partners for the show tonight. Sally from

Westport, whose feet spent more time on top of my feet than dancing between them. Pat from Cherry Hill, who seemed determined to cull me from the other hosts like a sheep dog culling her flock. Glynnis from Chicago, who really was quite a dancer and stood impatiently tapping her feet at the edge of the dance floor, each time I tried to work my magic with less than magical material, Glynnis trying to determine if it were permissible for her to cut in. I put an end to her anxieties by asking her for a second dance, once I'd been through the roster of others. I ended the night with Miranda from Baltimore, who after one dance, spent the rest of her ballroom time swallowing martinis as if they were after-dinner cordials instead of before-dinner . . . well martinis, dammit Fortunately, Miranda's cabin steward took over from me, when he saw how I was struggling with her coming down the corridor to her suite.

I take a final deep breath of the cool, clean sea air and turn to head back to my cabin to scribble some notes before the Mirandas from Baltimore or the Pats from Cherry Hill seem simply the exaggerated memories of some overnight dream sequence.

* * * * *

Andy Cross and I had agreed to meet for a late afternoon drink each day to talk about how it was going for me, whether I was getting the material I needed for my article and/or if there were anything he could do to help.

"Well," he said, "It sounds like you got a representative cross-section right out of the gate."

"Not quite as bad as pretending I could handle a horse for a story on the annual buffalo roundup at Custer State Park in South Dakota," I replied.

Cross laughed. "Well, you're still here and any accidents in South Dakota don't seem to have diminished your quick-step."

"Broken collarbone, long healed. My quickstep? Say, you been spying on me?"

"I have to make sure that agreeing to this will not cost me my job."

"Then, if you know the potential players, who should I be especially prepared to encounter?"

He paused a moment, pondering my question, then said, "The one to be aware of is Lucy Blakely. Not that she is anything but lovely and gracious."

"So why the warning?"

"It's not that she would be any kind of trouble, but she is our best customer. Very wealthy, ergo known to everyone at the top of our corporate ladder. Just want to make sure you understand the delicacy of any interaction with Lucy."

I studied him a moment. "Where have I heard her name before?" I asked.

"The supermarket tabloids? The society pages? Married to Alan Blakely? Investment banker?"

"Starting to come into focus. He in the messy aftermath of an affair. They in the middle of a contentious divorce. A lot of money involved in any settlement. That Lucille Blakely?"

"One and the same. This crossing is the first leg of our world cruise. Lucy does it with us every few years. This time is her first time as a soon-to-be ex-wife, with possibly even more money to spend with us. Told our CEO she really needed to get away, this time. Free herself from the tabloid pages. Free of the social circles that, for years, have done everything at the behest of Alan Blakely."

"And I should be concerned, why? I can't imagine she would have any interest in a dance host on a cruise ship."

"Right, mostly. But she is a very gregarious woman, very charming. And we're all confined here for the next seven days with no ports of call until we reach Southampton. Your paths may cross. *And,* you're a journalist, a member of the enemy from which she has fled."

"Someone like her would definitely enhance my article, but I try never to be exploitive and will definitely respect her space. I'm sure I despise the paparazzi almost as much as she does."

"Good enough," Cross said. "Well, your little drama is only one of many I need to tend to, so I'll take my leave."

"Tomorrow? Same time, same place?"

"For sure," he said, signed the check for the drinks, then rose from our table and left.

I headed back to my quarters to get some rest before dinner and that night's performance.

*   *   *   *   *

On the third night out, we were in heavy seas. An Atlantic hurricane had been tracking north from the Caribbean, skirted any significant North American landfall, and was pushed out into the Atlantic by a powerful high-pressure system forcing its way west across a cooling continent. The continent's good fortune became our bad one, as remnants of the storm created pitch and roll, which had passengers bouncing off walls. There were just a few takers at the ballroom, and each bailed after one dance. I was nursing an after-dinner bourbon and trying to focus my blurred vision on the band, which was going through a perfunctory set, as if there were anyone left on the dance floor, except a few dance hosts chatting with each other and a smattering of wifeless men among the rows of tables using the enforced solitude to have a drink undisturbed.

"Lucy Blakely," she said over my left shoulder, then came around to face me head on. She held out her hand.

I took it, of course, "Mike Rhodes. A pleasure, Mrs. Blakely."

"It's Lucy," she replied. "I've never enjoyed the pretentious formality of being Mrs. Blakely. No matter how much Alan did. And, in any event, I'm soon to shed the official Mrs. Blakely title. I've been replaced, this time, by a twenty-two-year-old intern, just out of university. All of which you may know already, if you've read any of New York's yellow journal tabloids."

She smiled and paused for just a second or two, as if to allow the last comment to sink in.

"Oh," I replied, "*that* Mrs. Blakely."

She nodded, then said, "May I join you . . . Mr. Rhodes?"

"It's Mike or if you insist upon the more formal, Michael," I said, motioning her to sit down. "Yellow journalism, hah? I haven't heard that term in decades. You don't look that old."

"Flattery will get you –"

"Nowhere?" I replied.

"Don't underestimate my wiles. You could get lucky. If you believe the tabloids."

"I tend to ignore them."

"That may place you at a disadvantage here."

"In that case, what can I get you to reclaim my advantage. Soften the edges."

She smiled. "They know what I like."

"But I don't. Just curious."

"Courvoisier. A sliver of Francophile heritage."

I waved toward one of the waiters. He just nodded. She raised two fingers and he headed toward the bar to order our drinks.

"Impressive," I said.

"Not really," she replied. "Just dozens of trips on these ships."

The waiter brought our two cognacs and we clinked glasses.

"You're one helluva dancer," she said, raising her glass in a mock toast.

I studied her a brief moment. "Just me trying to maintain my balance on a pitching dance floor that was doing my dance steps for me."

"I'm not talking about tonight."

I crinkled my eyebrows. "So, that was you who's been taking notes, each night, up in the dark seats, way up back?"

She couldn't restrain a laugh. "You're good at this repartee, aren't you?"

"I've had a lot of practice."

"Really."

She paused a moment, took a swallow of her drink, then, "Why are you here?" she asked.

I let out a laugh. "What? Are you the only one who can take some time off to cross the Atlantic with no good reason other than to enjoy it? How elitist."

"Touché."

"I write business books, OK? Almost always under contracts with companies or their senior executives. They pay me good money, then hand out the books to company execs, key clients, the business press, that sort of thing. When I'm done with one of those, I take some of the money I've earned and do something I've always wanted to do."

"Have you written anything I might have heard of?"

"Minimal general exposure outside of the markets represented by my subjects' companies. If any crossed your desk, the most likely would be 'Live Via Satellite,' about the company that produced the first orbiting geosynchronous communication satellites. It made some of the business best seller lists."

"I do know that book," she replied, a bit of delight in her voice as if she had just gotten the answer right on some TV quiz show. "Only because Alan created a mutual fund with companies involved in that satellite venture."

"I made some real money with that fund, but now I'm reluctant to ask you to thank him for me."

She smiled and nodded. "So," she continued, "we are both here for the same reason. Spending someone else's money on something frivolous."

I laughed and shook my head. "You're something, aren't you?"

"Yes," she said. "I am."

The repartee continued for another hour, with the seas getting even rougher, when, she drained the rest of her drink. "Want to find out how 'something' I *really* am?"

"Wa-what?" I said, astonished.

"Suddenly you're stammering like a little boy. Don't disappoint me, Michael. Finish your drink and let's get out of here."

$$* \quad * \quad * \quad * \quad *$$

"She was asking about you yesterday."

Andy Cross and I were having our afternoon cocktail session. The seas had calmed significantly. "I told her what you told me about writing business books. That was OK, right?"

I nodded, my head still a bit hammered from multiple, high-end drinks in her suite. "Yes, thank you."

"So, you met her?"

"Yeah. Yes . . . yes. We had a very pleasant conversation. Last night at the empty dance hall."

He raised his eyebrows. "Well," he said, "that didn't take long. I mean her finding you, as I had predicted."

"Well, now I know you sicked her on me."

"Oh, no. But when Lucy Blakely asks, we answer, and she asked about you."

"No worries. As you said, 'gracious, very charming.' Next time, *I'll* go looking for *her*."

His wry smile betrayed an understanding of Lucy that was way above a dancing host's pay grade, but after the previous night, I didn't give a damn.

He signed the check and left.

$$* \quad * \quad * \quad * \quad *$$

When you've been at this as long as I have, you find the best articles all but write themselves. Aside from the ladies, who, for the most part, were just on board for this transatlantic segment of the world cruise, my more significant subjects were my fellow dance hosts, most of whom were here for the duration, more than three months circling the globe. Although their employment did not include a salary, there was free room and board some pocket change for spending money and a chance to see a good deal of the world. Some had settled into this as a nice retirement pursuit, funded by lifelong contributions into their pension plans. Some were younger men, who signed on for segments of the world cruise as a lark. All were one kind of story

or another. As individuals, they were a string of dancing planets
orbiting the gentleman-hosting center of my article's solar
system.

The one who captured most of my interest was Charlie
Selfridge, a former English professor at the University of
Nebraska. Born a cornhusker, Charlie could not have been more
out of place in the Midwest prairie. He had spent most of his life
there yearning to experience cultures throughout the world, but
never having the level of resources to do anything but short-
term experiences between semesters. Although the hosts were
expressly forbidden contractually from having any kind of
romantic, let alone physical, relationships with passengers,
Charlie's other colleagues were all over describing how their
dance partners came on to them, either subtly, suggestively, or
even blatantly, thereby allowing them to reclaim some measure
of their fading sense of machismo. Often there was alcohol
involved on the part of the ladies. Charlie, however, played no
hand in that game.

Charlie's longer-term cohorts were convinced he was one of
those rare asexual individuals. He could form emotionally
intimate attachments with other people, but never sexual
relationships. Given that he didn't play the braggadocio games,
Charlie's acute powers of observation were of far more interest
to me. Also, given how many years he had remained a fixture as
one of the ship's dance hosts, I considered him my best source of
the material that would make it into my article. If Charlie was
never interested in any kind of sexual interaction, nonetheless I
found, he was always interested in conversational interaction.
He was a particularly astute observer of Lucy Blakely and he
liked to talk about her. His interest in her was partly because so
much of what he observed in others was superficial, while he
considered her genuinely true to herself and thereby an
engaging conversational partner.

"She's as gracious and lovely as any of us who know her long
term will tell you she is," he said over before-dinner martinis in
the cocktail lounge, "but . . ." He let the connective word just
hang there and didn't finish the sentence.

"But what?" I asked.

He just smiled and took a sip of his drink.

"What is this an exercise in one of your English classes about discovering the metaphorical component driving the plot's surface reality?"

"Well said, Michael," he replied. "You are definitely a potential A in this course."

"What I am definitely potential for is what comes after that 'but'."

"I like Lucy Blakely. Don't get me wrong. I like her a lot. We chat often and she'll always find some evenings to share a dance with me. It's just endlessly fascinating watching how she maneuvers through life."

"Maneuvers?"

"Oh, come on, Michael. You don't become one of the richest women in the world without knowing how to ply dangerous seas."

"Now with the nautical references? For Christ's sake, Charlie, you're from Nebraska."

"Yeah, but I been a mariner for years, *matey*."

"Groan. Back to Mrs. Maneuverer, please."

He took another sip and studied me for a moment. "You're not going to write anything nasty about Lucy, are you?"

"Why? Are there nasty things to write about her?"

"No," he replied without hesitation. "There are not."

"Besides," I countered, "the tabloids have covered, pretty extensively, what they find particularly nasty."

"True, but I've read nothing about her onboard maneuverings."

"Again, with the maneuverings?"

He laughed. "What I can tell you, based upon sharing many voyages with her, she is an extremely intelligent individual. On a world cruise, we become a neighborhood. For three months there is a lot of interaction between staff and the passengers who remain on board for the full circumnavigation. And she has done the world cruise multiple times, going back to the earliest years in her marriage. I've shared a number of those voyages with her. We have had many conversations about many subjects. She is extremely well read. She and I have had multiple discussions about English literature that no one, without a degree in the subject, could handle as well as she does."

"So, your interest is purely academic subject matter?"

Again, he studied me quietly. "Is this how the crack reporters work? Hammer away at a poor interview subject until he opens up on what you're really after?"

"Just making conversation here . . . matey. Just trying to hold my own with you."

"I like you, Michael," he replied, "but I don't really know you at all. I've had very little experience with journalists. Academics, yes. Journalists, no. I don't want to say something that hurts someone I care about, someone who is the subject of so much nasty press."

"I don't write those kinds of articles, Charlie. Besides, the women on board are of only passing interest for my purposes. It's you guys who are my real subjects."

"So, you will say nasty things about me?"

"Absolutely."

We both had a good laugh and finished our drinks, then headed to the staff dining room for dinner. None of our colleagues were present, which left Charlie and I to a bit more uninterrupted conversation and I was not quite finished picking his brain about Lucy Blakely.

"To your point, Lucy approached me during that terrible weather, when there were so few people in the ballroom, and we had a brief conversation. My reaction now is she was all the nice things you've been saying about her, but . . ."

"Uh-oh. Look out, Michael. That's how it starts."

"What? How what starts?"

He paused a moment. "The Austrian prince on the first world cruise. The son of the German industrialist on the second."

"And me? No known pedigree?"

"I'd place you in the category of the handsome Filipino who was a crooner with the orchestra a few years back."

"And?"

"She just likes you."

"And? Has any of that ever made it into the tabloids?"

"Not to my knowledge."

"I'm miffed. Why hasn't that stuff?"

"From my observations, I'd guess discretion is the essential membership requirement among the super-rich elite, including Austrian princes and the sons of German industrialists."

"Jesus, wouldn't this be an intelligence gold strike for her husband's lawyers to use against her in the divorce suit?"

"Hey, don't even think about going there. That could be very destructive on so many levels."

"My writing has nothing to do with lawyers, Charlie. Just wondering."

"Then I'd advise not just wondering about it, even to yourself."

I let out a deep rush air. "My work is exhausting, Charlie, but someone has to do it."

He stared at me a moment, then said, "I've said enough about Lucy. I fear what I've said, and left unsaid, will become too interesting for you not to pursue."

"Not to worry. Sometimes I get so wrapped up in merely observing what's happening around me, I feel like everything is a story. But I don't do that kind of story and never will."

"I see."

I stared at him a moment; then suddenly was hit with a realization I didn't see coming. "*You* are writing about all this, aren't you? What is it, your great American novel? All these voyages, all these people morphing into characters in *your* opus. Lucy, of course. Now even me."

"So," he replied, picking up a menu, "what looks good for dinner?"

*　*　*　*　*

When you've had a romantic interlude, facilitated by copious amounts of alcohol – God love it – alcohol makes all of it seem so right. But then, you can never be quite sure how your next interaction with the party of the second part is going to go. And, since I was on a cruise ship, albeit with some fifteen hundred fellow passengers aboard, it was still a small community, given that there were only nine decks and perhaps a dozen public rooms, indoors and out, wherein to hide yourself. And so it was that I opted for the cocktail lounge as my morning retreat, feeling just a cup of coffee and my notebooks would provide all the companionship I'd require, and a cocktail lounge would be a safe haven away from all those piling it on at the breakfast buffet. Alas, she found me, anyway. By now, I would have to accept that as the ersatz commandress of the staff corps, she would have intelligence outposts throughout the ship. I would have guessed even my cabin may have surveillance cameras.

"Ah, there you are, Mr. Rhodes," she said as she approached my table. "It appears you dropped your bowtie outside my quarters when you were kind enough to escort me back there the other evening."

"Oh," I replied, "I was wondering what happened to that. It's my favorite. Thank you for your kindness. Can I offer you a cup of coffee and some sweet rolls?"

"A cup of tea would be nice" she said, at the same time motioning to the attendant, who already started brewing some for her. She took the seat opposite me.

I closed my journal and placed it on the table between us.

"Another business book?" she asked.

"Nope, just some observations for my best-selling novel."

"Do tell. What are some of your other novels? I'll have some serious down time over the next three months. Perhaps you have one or two you can lend me."

The waiter came over with her tea and placed it on the table before her. She blew lightly on it and took a sip.

I looked at her, smiled and shook my head.

"So, how are you, Michael?" she asked. "I'm feeling pretty well, myself, should you want to inquire."

I couldn't resist a broad smile. "Who the hell are you?" I asked. "And what planet are you from? You've given me plenty to last me for the final few days of this voyage, but lo, here you are again."

"Enough to last? Are you filling some kind of quota?"

"Of course not. But I'm guessing you have an ability to create experiences that somehow seem unreal. Unreal, but absolutely lovely. Am I wrong about that?"

"Wow," she said, "lovely. Are you sure you should confine your work to business books? Boring old business books."

"Excuse me," I replied. "Nothing *I* ever write is boring."

"I'm sure." She took another sip of her tea. "How the hell are you, Michael? May I call you Michael?"

"Absolutely not, Lucille. I'd rather the Lucy/Mike nomenclature we settled on lo that hundred years ago. And to answer your question, I'm doing fine, Lucy. And you?"

"Couldn't be better."

"I'm happy," I said, smiling warmly. "You sure know how to make a guy's evening."

"It only works when I'm with a special guy."

"OK. I throw myself on the mercy of the court. If you're trying to make me feel any better than you have already done, then I'm not sure I have the energy to resist."

"Pity," she said, "for I do have some free time after the dinner at the captain's table this evening. And I see you, too, are on the guest list."

"Right, and it does relieve me of my dancing duties tonight."

"So . . ."

I smiled. "Well, these past five minutes have been all the time I can hold out from your offer to get together."

"Then, see you at dinner."

She took a few more sips of her tea, rose from the table and departed. I went back to my notes.

* * * * *

And then she started to get strange on me. I have found women tended to do that, especially women with whom I have had intimate contact. With Lucy, it began during that same afternoon, when I saw her and Charlie Selfridge talking, while sharing tea, in a small lounge adjacent to the first class dining room. As I stood in the entryway surveying the room, Lucy looked briefly in my direction, seemed to note my presence but made no gesture for me to come join them. In fact, she rearranged her seating position to turn her back toward me. I did an about face, a bit awkwardly, and left.

That evening, when I entered the dining room for dinner, as I neared the captain's table, Lucy stood up abruptly, announced she was suddenly feeling ill and excused herself. She walked briskly by me, without acknowledging me in any way. After dinner, I called her suite and left a message inquiring how she was feeling and asking if I could be of any help, but she left no return message. When I tried to approach Charlie to see if he knew what was troubling her, he found reasons to be unavailable.

By the remaining full day of the voyage, I was chalking up my brief Lucy Blakely experience as just another of the inexplicable encounters I have had with women over my decades of wandering. Nonetheless, this turn of events was bothering me more than others. I didn't expect my experience with Lucy to amount to much more than a brief interlude, a warm friendship we had had during one of those Atlantic crossings, which provided fodder for so many stories by so many writers I admired during the days before jet travel badly diminished the crossings. And then, as I passed one of the doors, which opened out onto the Promenade Deck, I saw her, leaning against the railing and staring out at the ocean, her hair slightly bouncing about a bit in a light breeze.

I approached, moving one of the deck chairs between her and me, to make just enough of a sound so as not to startle her when I got close. She turned from the railing, saw my approach, then shook her head ever so slightly.

"What is it?" I asked. "How have I offended you?"

"You said you wrote business books. You didn't tell me you wrote newspaper articles and were writing a syndicated piece about your experiences on this trip. And, we know, don't we, that one of your quote 'experiences' is me."

Now, I shook my head. "I see. So, Charlie has filled your head with his take on what I am up to."

She said nothing, but her lack of rebuttal was enough.

"I should have pegged him for a world-class gossip. He defined you as, and I quote, a 'maneuverer,' but that was to throw me off the scent, while he fomented a drama of his own creation. For one of the very few times in my life, I let my naiveté get the better of me. When he spoke about you, I have to admit I had a very keen interest, but my interest grew more personal than anything I would do professionally. Lucy, yes getting to know you really has given me what would be material for perhaps the yellowest journalism . . ." I paused a moment, "that I am never going to write. Not happening."

She looked at me with the slightest hint of a questioning expression.

"Please, Lucy. I've got to believe that even in the short time we've been together we've gotten to know each other well enough to form character judgments."

A smile formed at the corners of her mouth.

Finally, she said, "After Charlie quote, 'let it slip' about the article you're writing, I've been running the movie reel in my head of the time we've spent together. While it includes some scenes that could be very damaging for me, you bear no resemblance to the tabloid reporters who have hounded me."

"Thank you."

"Can I trust you not to betray my feelings nor the intimacies we've shared?"

"Of course you can. I *am* a journalist. The call of my profession is to seek out relevant stories and place them before the public to evaluate. But part of the code, which many of my unscrupulous colleagues seem to have forgotten, is we don't betray a trust, in my case even an unspoken trust. I won't do that, Lucy. If you like, I'll sign a nondisclosure agreement."

She smiled warmly again. "No," she said. "That won't be necessary. I don't need one more reason to see my attorney."

I returned the smile but held it a bit too long.

"What is it?" she asked. "I'm sorry, I don't know you that long, but I *do* know that look when I see it.

I laughed. "This *could* make a wonderful story someday, don't you think? Camouflaged as fiction. With your permission, of course. All names changed to protect the guilty."

Her smile widened. "Well, guilty *is* a role I've been accused of by batteries of Alan's lawyers."

"A character in a work of fiction, a first for you, yes?"

"On the contrary. Many times, according to my soon-to-be ex-husband."

We both laughed.

"So, you're intrigued. I can see it on *your* face," I said, my smile brightening. "It'll be a reason for us to keep in touch."

Her smile widened to challenge mine.

We paused during one of those lulls, when all that needed to be said had been said. We regarded each other with a warmth that had been a leitmotif since we'd first met. I broke the brief silence.

"There's nothing in my terms of agreement that prohibits me from being the one asking for a dance."

I opened my arms. She folded into them. We began to dance a slow foxtrot, to the accompaniment of the rhythmic roll of the sea.

"Your hair smells wonderful, Mrs. Blakely, just a hint of sea salt."

"Well then, thank you, Mr. Rhodes," she said.

"Well then, thank *you*, Mrs. . . .

[CTL Find] Bartlett

[CTL Replace] Blakely . . .

❧

EQUILIBRIUM

A billow of breeze
Flaps the cloth at her knees
The angular light warms her cheek.
The salt-scarred terra cotta
Licks her feet.

Even for a setting with dozens of sailing craft, berthed in the marina in front of the outdoor dining area, at the Road Town Harbour Hotel, where I was enjoying breakfast, as the sun rose higher above the Sir Francis Drake Channel, the brigantine schooner coasting between the mouth of Road Harbour and tiny Bellamy Cay was an attention-getter.

       chop up run-on sent very late to "attention-getter."
The multi-masted sailing ship had to be at least eighty, ninety feet and sleek as an ~~outstretched eel~~. '~~53 Corvette~~ ~~P-80 Shooting Star~~ SPEEDING BULLET!!! Outstretched eel?

I looked up from my journal a moment, studied the action just beyond the mouth of the harbor, then continued.

The schooner had no sooner (restructure the inadvertent rhyme) dropped anchor, when a dingy was lowered over the side. A crew member slid down a ladder into the small boat, took a suitcase from another crewman up top, a backpack held down to him from a woman on deck, then assisted the woman down the ladder and into a seat in the stern. The crewman cranked the engine and headed for the hotel's marina.

I closed my notebook and watched as the small craft, in a long, lazy arc, approached the transient dock, several yards in front of where I was seated. After placing the suitcase and backpack carefully on the wharf, the crewman assisted the woman up, then headed his dingy back toward the schooner.

The woman slung her backpack over one shoulder, lifted her suitcase, walked up to the restaurant entrance, and stood almost directly in front of my table. Dropping the suitcase alongside her and shifting her sunglasses to the top of her head, she seemed to be studying the lay of the land. She was medium height, her body language, her clothes, even her expensive-looking suitcase, projecting a kind of understated elegance. Her blond hair was cut and coiffed into layers that would look right where e'er they fell, in whatever breeze. Fair skin and blue eyes gave off a decidedly Nordic look. These were all characteristics I generally found attractive, however, there was something about the way she embodied them, which said her physical appearance would play but one part in what defined her.

"Reception is up that path directly behind me," I offered.

"Oh, I don't have a reservation," she replied with a smile that brightened her eyes, which now I could make out as strikingly pale blue.

"In that case," I said, "do you have time for a cup of coffee, while you consider your next move?"

"Black," she said, lifting and placing her suitcase across the armrests of a seat alongside mine and taking the seat opposite.

"Michael Rhodes." I offered my hand.

She took it. "Tereza Grymes."

"Nice suitcase," I said. "Louis Vuitton?"

"The captain was a generous man."

I called the waiter over and ordered her coffee and one more for me as well. He brought a cup and saucer for her, filled her cup, then refilled mine.

"Breakfast?" I asked.

"Had it on board. A farewell repast among friends."

"Very nice."

"But thank you for offering."

There was the loud noise of a hefty nautical engine starting up nearby, then a launch carrying about a half-dozen passengers pulled out into the harbor and headed for the schooner.

"Your ride is picking up some replacements," I said, adding some brown sugar to my coffee and taking a sip.

"They're headed back to Cape Town," she replied. "The schooner takes them across to these islands after Christmas each year, then ferries them home in time for Easter. I managed to latch onto this unique ferry service."

"Impressive. Courageous. OK, daring."

"Had had my fill of Cape Town." She blew some air across her cup and took a sip. "Very nice coffee."

"Costa Rican. The main reason I stay at this hotel."

She smiled warmly. "I don't think so."

"Well, one of the reasons." I took another sip, then, "So, whoa, wait a minute, you rode that beauty across from South Africa. That's gotta be a long, challenging sea voyage."

"We island-hopped along the way."

"There's no hopping until you reach the Leeward Islands and by then you're almost here."

"Came across well southeast of the Leewards. We made a few stops along the coast of Brazil before heading north into the Caribbean."

"I'm trying to wrap my head around all that time in open ocean."

"Accommodations aboard the ship were quite nice. Predictably, we had a number of rough stretches. Anyway, I like ocean voyages."

The brief repartee had nonetheless afforded me enough time to finish my coffee, usually a multi-cup experience each morning.

"You inhaled that coffee," she remarked.

"I told you, Costa Rican. Heavenly."

She stared at me a moment as if trying to discern some deeper meaning in our casual exchanges about the coffee, then, "Let me have your coffee cup," she said.

"What?"

She reached out her hand.

"There's very little coffee left."

"I'm not going to drink your dregs," she said with a laugh. "I'm curious about something."

I stared at her questioningly.

"Your cup?" She persisted.

I handed her the cup. She took hers off its saucer and placed it alongside, then turned my cup upside down on the dish.

I looked at her quizzically, but she ignored me, staring down at the cup and tapping the bottom lightly a few times. Then she turned it over and began studying it.

"Hmmm," she uttered, holding it so I could see inside the cup, then pointing at one of four threads of coffee that gravity had pulled toward the lip while she'd had it overturned in her saucer. "You see how this thread widens as it approaches the lip of the cup, it means --"

"Whoa," I replied, "you're not going to tell me where I've come from by examining tiny streaks of coffee in the cup I was just drinking from? And, I presume where, I'm headed?"

"Look at this one thread," she said, ignoring my comment. "Your horizons keep widening as you've grown older. You're a traveler, an explorer."

"OK," I answered, "good one. But that could be an easy call. Why else would I be here?"

"You're here alone. You travel alone."

"I could be here on business."

"Are you?"

"I'm a writer. I travel alone on assignments."

"Part of the answer as to why you are a lone traveler is in this thread, right alongside the other. You see how it ends, almost exactly halfway to the lip?"

"Yes."

"You lack companionship."

"I don't know. You're here now, aren't you?"

"Touché."

She studied the lines further, then, "this one's worrisome. Or maybe just sorrowful."

I looked into the cup.

"You see how this thread is the opposite of the first one that was widening toward the lip? This one narrows. And you see how it's broken. I'd say a broken home as a child."

"Nope," I said, shaking my head. "Not so."

"Then some other broken relationship. One that was hurtful in terms of what you lost."

I just stared at her.

"Your marriage?"

"Yes," I said, "Look, do we get to do your coffee cup next?"

"I can't read my own."

"So I get to do it?"

She didn't answer.

"OK," she said finally, "truthfully, what I am finding is pretty generic, pretty predictable in the lives of most people."

"So what about you?" I questioned. "Where's your broken thread?"

"Fair enough," she replied, "but first let's see if there's anything else."

"OK . . . I guess."

She picked up my cup again. Once again, she seemed to intensely study some aspect of what she was seeing.

"What?" I asked, now hopelessly hooked into this whole exercise.

"This line," she replied, "very unusual."

"How so?"

"The squiggles? Very unusual. Gravity tends to pull all the threads in relatively straight lines."

"And?"

"It's closest to the cup handle. That's the line that generally signifies equilibrium. Yours wavers. I don't want to wander too far out of my zone here, but I'd say you are in a great struggle with yourself. That is, you're in a struggle to find yourself."

"OK, again pretty generic. Aren't we all on that quest?"

"Yes, but it's a matter of degree. You seem a captive of the search, almost unaccepting of when you're presented with strong indications of where you have really landed. Unaccepting even when you're in a place where you'd otherwise want to be. You are not comfortable in stasis. That original finding of you as the traveler, the explorer, it seems that you see the quest as the end in itself. Not accepting when you find a landing zone."

"This is exhausting," I said. "I don't work this hard when I'm fending off my therapist."

"I rest my case."

"OK, then, what about you? You're traveling alone. Hell, you've crossed the ocean in a sailboat. Where's your home? Was it a broken one?"

"Kinesis is my equilibrium."

"Kinesis? Equilibrium? How can perpetual motion provide equilibrium?"

"Equilibrium is not simply a matter of a lack of motion. It's a balance of powers. In simple terms, a comfort zone. I am

comfortable in the movement. Your movement is only a means
to an end. Stasis is your equilibrium, but for some reason you
fight it. You're uncomfortable whenever you get there, when
you're simply in it. That's why the turmoil in the coffee threads.
You and I are both wanderers, but for me it is my path; for you
it's how you escape an equilibrium you don't want to accept.

"Well," I said, "this explorer has to wander back to my place
and get some work done."

I started to rise, but she made no move to get up.

"Where to from here?" I queried.

"Don't know. Haven't really thought it through short term."

"I assume you got off here for a reason."

"Yes, but it's just a short stay. I have a contract as a hostess
on the Royal Cruise Lines Royal Duchess. I'll meet the ship when
it arrives tomorrow. She spends one day in port here in Tortola,
then island hops the West Indies before passing through the
Panama Canal for a voyage across the Pacific."

"So then you don't have accommodations for tonight?"

"I'll manage," she said.

I took a breath, studied her for a moment. "Look," I said, "I
have a suite at the hotel here, two bedrooms, kitchenette, living
room. You're welcome to the spare bedroom for tonight."

She returned the studied look.

"No unsavory expectations," I said. "I won't encroach on
your space. You don't even need to make the bed in the
morning. I have maid service. It's a hotel, after all."

Her look dissolved into a warm smile.

"How can I pass up such a generous offer?"

I returned the smile. "May I get your bag, ma'am?"

"But of course, kind sir," she said, rising from her chair.

* * * * *

While she spent the afternoon exploring Road Town, the
islands' capital on Tortola, I worked on one of a series of articles
I was writing about the British Virgin Islands. My concentration
upon my article was redirected frequently by thoughts of her . . .

158

When she returned from her explorations, she accepted my offer to join me for dinner.

We dined at the second floor, al fresco restaurant above the harbor, as the sun dropped behind the islands in the Drake Channel and the sails of the charter yachts filled with orange light as they returned to their moorings. I told her that, as a journalist, I was incurably curious about the lives of the people I'd met, and asked her forgiveness in advance over the endless stream of questions I'd toss at her. Nonetheless, she was very free about describing what I found to be a fascinating family history.

"My father had been a cadet in an Italian naval officer training school, when Italy fell to the allies in 1943," she said. "He was conscripted, unwillingly, by the Nazi army retreating north through Italy from their losses in Africa. He hated the fascists who'd taken over his country and their affiliation with the Nazis; there was no way he was going to fight for Hitler. His captors were not pleased, so he was sent to a prison camp in the Sudetenland, now part of Czechoslovakia. When the camp was liberated in 1945, he spent two months in Prague, living with my mother, before arranging transport back to his hometown in the Tyrol Mountains of North Italy, leaving behind his common law war bride and me on the way."

"Well, I guess that explains the blond hair and blue eyes."

"You're very perceptive."

"You damn well know your eyes are hard to ignore."

"I thought you said you'd be burying me in questions, not interrupting my story?"

"Proceed."

"My mother was Romani, a Gypsy, but descendent of the Vikings on her mother's side. Ergo the pale blue eyes, wise ass."

"Sorry."

"She survived the Nazi annihilation of the Gypsies in Czechoslovakia because of her clearly Nordic complexion and her adoption of the family name Grymes, from the Scandinavian side of her ancestry. She'd been working as a hotel maid in Prague when my father got there."

"Wait, Grimes, is a very British name."

"When spelled with an i. My mother spelled it: g r Y m e s. Very Nordic."

"Romani/Gypsy, ergo your fortune telling."

"Ergo."

Thus we traded life stories for several hours, over dinner and two bottles of wine, she pressing me on my journeys to destinations she'd yet to explore; me proceeding with my often lengthy accounts thereof, until the waitstaff was getting restless and the manager finally, diplomatically, explaining they were having to close things up. I told the manager if he could retrieve one more bottle of wine and add it to my bill, we'd be out of there as soon as he returned.

"On the house," he said with a broad smile, and we departed.

Settled into the living room at my suite, it seemed we were lost in more accounts of our pasts that would travel well into our futures. There was an almost reflexive dynamic to the ongoing stories .

"I'm curious about your near perfect command of English."

"*Near* perfect?"

"Slight, not-quite-placeable accent, although very sexy."

"Sexy?"

I smiled and nodded. "Yes, sexy. So how does a Czech in a Russian controlled country learn English."

"I'd been permitted to take English in school to get a job as a translator for the few British businessmen who were permitted in Czechoslovakia during the Russian occupation. Our Russian overseers approved and were always subjecting us to debriefings. However, one of the businessmen, for whom I translated regularly, managed to secretly arrange a British passport for me and passage to the UK, where he set me up in an apartment. I knew I had to escape that arrangement and faded into the British populace. My basic understanding of how British business worked, via all my translating, got me lower level jobs in business and finance, but I was terminally bored. Thereby began my wanderings.

"Sounds like a plot for a spy movie. We could collaborate on the screenplay."

"I'm more interested in *your* accent."

"My . . . accent? What? You've adopted some of that English snobbery about American English?

"A bit of the . . . guttural," she persisted.

"Guttural? Really?"

"Not really," she said with a laugh. "Just my parry to the nerve of your questioning my accent."

"Queens," I said.

"Queen? What about the queen?"

"Not the damned queen," I said with a laugh. "Queens," "New York City's quintessentially suburban borough of Queens."

"Never been there."

"If you've ever landed at JFK, you've been there."

"On my list."

I was quiet for a moment, my alcohol-stimulated mind, wandering back to the days of my youth and early adulthood. "Some of my fondest memories are from there."

"Hmmm," she replied.

"What?"

"Sweethearts? There must have been sweethearts."

"Yeah, sure. But nothing ever serious. Just a kind of warmup for the dance. I left in my early twenties."

"I don't know," she countered, appearing to resume that penetrating look she had used on me since she first walked into my life. "I don't know."

I had no reply and suddenly was feeling the crash from all the wine coming on with increasing intensity.

"I'm sorry," I said, "I feel myself rapidly running out of energy. And I don't want to start slurring my words and ruining a pretty wonderful day and evening."

"Me, as well," she replied. "Thank *you* for a most interesting day and evening."

We retired to our separate bedrooms.

* * * * *

I awoke from one of those alcohol-induced comas by what sounded like a muffled attempt at my name. My addled brain, begged to fall back into the neutrality of sleep, but then there it was again: "Michael." This time barely above a whisper.

I shook what few cobwebs were still loose and functional in my brain and focused on the doorway to my bedroom, where she stood, lit softly by the security lamp outside my window.

"Tereza?"

"Michael," she said, "I'm sorry to disturb you. I had a vivid dream I was once again in the throes of brutality of the Russian occupation. I'm terrified to go back to my bed and back to the horror of those days. Would you hold me?"

"Of course," I replied.

She walked softly to my bedside.

"May I?" she asked, as she lifted my blanket.

"Of course. Of course." I slid over a bit to make room for her.

She got in, folding immediately into the safety of my embrace.

"Thank you," she said, gripping me tightly and nuzzling her head in the crook of my neck.

* * * * *

What alternative moments of sleep I got during the rest of our night together managed to nullify what had been the cinderblock effects of my hangover between moments of sheer loveliness.

162

The sun was considerably higher in the morning than my usual hour to begin writing fortified by the parade of my morning cups of coffee, as she crossed the threshold into the kitchenette where I sat at the table. I closed my notebook.

"Sleep well?" I offered.

"Yes," she replied. "After that . . . interruption? I slept very well."

"Hey," I said, "I was the interrup-*tee* not the interrup-*tor*. Nonetheless, now I'm battling recriminations. After all, I did promise to be good."

"And you were very good," she said with a warm smile as she walked to the counter where the coffee pot stood. "Any coffee left?"

"Should be. Cups are in the cabinet just above."

She took down a cup, poured some coffee then sat opposite me at the small round table.

"Oh," she said, pointing to my hands folded atop my notebook. "I didn't mean to interrupt . . . again. I can go sit out on the patio. Looks like a beautiful morning."

"You're not interrupting. Were it not for enforced breaks in my workday, I'd probably be writing nonstop from wakeup to bedtime. A good deal of it just meaningless observations and fanciful meanderings."

"I'm sure that's a bit of an exaggeration, but thank you for excusing this interruption."

She took a sip, than stared at me through a very warm expression.

"What?" I asked. "Why that look?"

"You have very soft hands," she replied.

"OK . . .?"

"Last night. Very soft hands. It was a very warm experience."

"OK? Now you're embarrassing me."

She took another sip, then, "May I see your hands?"

I looked at her quizzically, but responded by holding out my hands.

"Turn them over, please."

I complied.

"Let me see the left one."

"It never knows what the right one is doing," I said with a laugh, then offered my hand. She took it and studied it for a few moments.

"Would you like me to pour some coffee in it to accentuate the threads?" I asked.

"Very funny."

"And?"

"Your life line is long, but faint."

"Which means?"

"This journey of exploration, through which you have defined your life? It's there. It's long. But it's weak."

I smiled and shook my head. "You're just trying to support your coffee cup reading."

"Well, there it is. The supporting evidence. The heart line is the one I find most interesting, however."

"I'm afraid to ask."

"Your love line -- more accurately your search for love -- runs in an arc similar to your life line, although the two arcs concave away from each other, as if they are magnetic poles pushing in opposite directions. Then, what I find most unusual in your heart line is the breaks. Most unusual."

"I cut my hand badly a number of years ago, grabbing for a ledge on a climb up a cliffside. That may explain it."

"The heart line is strong at the origination point, then bumps along as it journeys through life, until it begins to diverge from your life line."

"Two marriages may account for the bumps."

"Yes, they would do it. But it's that early strength in the heart line I find most interesting, especially when compared to the line's weakness beyond the bumps."

"Your analysis, please."

"Difficult, but if I had to, I'd say your true love connection occurred early in your life, but either you didn't recognize it, or you chose to dismiss it."

"Well, that's very disappointing. Do I tie a weight to an ankle and jump into the Drake Channel or . . . I don't know. Do what?"

"I'm not trying to find some sign of hope here," she said, "just reporting what I see." She took another searching look at my left hand, "but one of the results of that injury is that the arc of your love line is redirected in some odd way, as if it is trying to turn."

"Can I have my hand back?" I asked.

"Of course."

She looked at me and smiled warmly.

"Our . . . encounter last night was just one more way station in your life," she said. "Don't misinterpret this. It was an act of love, very different from a purely libido-driven encounter. There was a real exchange of love there. But now I read it as one more experience in your search for love. It was an experience that was lovely for me. But -- and please don't misinterpret this -- it was not helpful in moving you toward your destiny."

"I don't know what to say."

"No need to pursue this, Michael. You're a lovely man. Know that. I wish you well on your path to equilibrium.

* * * * *

She spent the morning on the patio behind my suite, most of it beneath the shade of a tamarind tree, alternately rising and walking the short slope down to the Drake Channel to wet her feet in its almost indescribably clear waters, their light blue tint above the pinks and yellows of the coral reefs just beyond the shore.

I sat at the kitchen table facing the archway to the patio, catching glimpses of her as she made her short journeys down to the water. We both seemed to project contentment just to be in each other's neighborhood. None of the torrents of words, which had defined our brief relationship, were necessary.

At one point, just up the slope from the waterline, she stood with her back against a pole supporting the canopy outside the door to the patio, luxuriating in the cool breeze off the water and whatever thoughts it was inspiring in that brain of hers, which I was convinced never rested. In this case however, it appeared that she had achieved some level of the equilibrium that she said I would achieve in stasis, as if she were showing me how it was done.

I stopped scribbling lines in my story. Instead, I wrote:

> *A billow of breeze*
> *Flaps the cloth at her knees,*
> *The angular light warms her cheek.*
> *The salt-scarred terra cotta*
> *Licks her feet.*
> *Equilibrium*

A blast of the horn of the Royal Duchess put an end to her reverie.

She gathered herself up from her perch on the patio and came inside.

"Well, Michael," she said, "Gotta go."

"I'll give you a lift to the port, of course."

"Thank you. That would be nice."

At portside, we located the gangway to the crew deck. I carried her Louis Vuitton suitcase to it.

We embraced, then couldn't resist exchanging a kiss.

"It's been very nice to know you," I said. "And somehow I feel I *do* know you."

She just smiled for a moment, then said, "I've been thinking about what I saw in your heart line."

"Really?" I replied. "Really? What about it?"

"The sign that your true love connection occurred early in your life. Life's principal objective is to reconnect the yin and yang, most often across years and many miles. In your case, it occurred very early on, as if the connection had been established, perhaps even reestablished, in a remnant of the eternal present, which was still flickering at your landing here on our planet. Now I see *that* is what I saw."

A shiver raced through my body. It almost staggered me.

"I ..." but I had no words to finish with.

"Good-bye, Michael," she said, then turned and started up the gangway.

NOTEBOOKS

Caffé de Perugia: Mid-afternoon snack. Bel paese cheese; warm, crusty slices of bread; ripest, sweetest black figs and a fine chianti. Sunny day, cloudless sky, light breeze.

The highlight of this summer's Northern Italian Jazz Festival for me was last night's Armstrong/Holiday Classical Jazz Orchestra, 12 pieces performing dead-on versions of Louis Armstrong and Billie Holiday songs, fully deserving of the

Look at those three. Extras in a Fellini movie? Especially the
one on the left. Fashionably dressed on this warmish Italian
afternoon. All three sipping an Italian red, holding the wineglass
stems with the delicacy of aristocrats.
Where was I?

*The jazz orchestrations would have been fodder for my father
in our battles over the supremacy of his music versus my
allegiance to the new rock 'n' roll of my youth. My music's
growing dominance of the radio airwaves had exiled my father to
listening to old '78 rpm records of his songs because his favorite
radio networks had been taken over by fast-talking DJs, spinning
just my rock 'n' roll. My father would lambast me for my bands,
who were even filling the musical guest appearances on the TV
variety shows, shaggy-haired groupings he felt should have
remained consigned to the cellars or garages where they
rehearsed. "Do you call that music?" Whatever I called it, his
broken-record response was always that it couldn't compare to
the velvety sounds of tuxedo-clad musicians in big bands and their
sophisticated artistry. "You can't jump up and down and play
anything good on those wood-plank guitars they swirl around and
swat at." OK, admittedly, now in my let's just say later middle-aged
years –*

Did that one on the left just sneak a smile at me? Is she only
pretending to listen to her two companions?
I raise my glass to take another sip, hold it straight in front
of me for just an instant, using it as a transparent shield through

which to establish eye contact. For just an instant. Did she? For just that instant? She rejoins their conversation. Oh God, Michael, not again.

Back to the music review.

This year, I found the other performances formulaic: progressive trios – piano, bass, drums; or replace piano with guitar or vibes; maybe add a sax – not progressive. Their repertoires would have passed muster as "progressive" maybe forty years ago. Then the dissonant, atonal groups, each playing their own solo, all at the same time, within a performance that bore no resemblance to anything –

I stop writing. It's boring me. Once past the Classical Jazz Orchestra owning their genre's history, the rest of it is the same shit as last year, disguised as innovative. The potential for drama *here* is a far more interesting dynamic. I raise my head slowly. She is saying something to her two companions. One attempts to look over in my direction while trying not to make apparent what she is doing. She gives up and says something to the other two.

I need an elixir.

Where the hell is it? I rummage through my overstuffed backpack. Need a reminder of what not to. It's all there in the first new notebook I bought right after I got the backpack. Squeezed in now, ancient history, somewhere down there in one of the innumerable pockets these packs contain to keep you from finding anything quickly. Giraffe on the book cover for no good reason. Never been to Africa. Been to a lot of places, but never been to Africa. Here it is. Leaf through the pages to . . . here. The page pasted in. Carefully typed, cut to size, then pasted in. Some need to preserve the words. Need to remind myself that I never learn. I take a breath. A deep breath. I lay the old notebook down on the table.

This year's festival even expanded the concept of jazz to include –

Fuck it. I take up the old notebook, return to the pasted-in page and the memory of a conversation . . .

"My editor, the one who had published many of my travel articles, she kept trying to make me stop. Her recurring theme: 'Why do you need to transform some observed reality into an alternative reality of your own making? I pay you good money to deal with reality.'"

"She's right, you know. That other prose you're writing isn't real. It didn't happen."

"That's what they call fiction, mon docteur."

"Of course. But you write about it like it's what actually happened."

"Fiction, doctor. Fiction."

"But when you write it, it somehow seems real to you."

"It is real to me, isn't that why I'm here?"

He studies me a moment, as if my side has scored a point. He now needs a way forward.

"Tell me about it," he parries, "the real versus the surreal. The . . . fiction."

"It's all in my notebooks."

"Your self-analyses, then."

"No, my fiction, dammit. My *stories*."

"So, tell me about them."

"Why don't I just bring the notebooks. I'll bring them, the notebooks."

Instead of the notebooks, I condensed the most biting passages down to one page. I just brought the one-page condensed version. I even gave it a title. "Stark Remarks from Disasters Past." Purposely rhymed. Have a little fun with it. Fun fiction.

Siobhan: "I had only prayed that you had felt the same, Michael. Perhaps it was merely my pathetic need to have had you feel as I did. My belief that I could not have experienced such a connection if you had not as well."

Aldina: "You're a sweetheart, Michael. I have nothing but warm feelings for you, but we are from two different worlds. You could never live here, in my world; I could never live there, in yours."

Gabby: "Who are they all? What is the meaning of all their lives? Tell me, have you ever written about me?" "No," I answered, feebly. "Hah!" she blurted. "I don't believe you." "Nothing I'm happy with," I said, again lamely.

Laura: "Let's just say you gave me a year of joy, Michael, and leave it at that. Can't you see what you did for me? I love you, Michael, but I'm trapped."

> Contemplative look. "I see," he says.
> "You see? What do you see?"
> "It's not about what I see."
> "What am *I* supposed to see?"
> "You know the rules. I ask the questions."
> I nod.
> "So, what have you learned from all that?"
> "..."

Circumstance will be my salvation, this time, right? There are three of them. No way to section her off from the other two. She'll leave with her two companions.

Back to my writing.

This year's festival even expanded the concept of jazz to include more blues, even some hip-hop scat with a horn section. OK, so now we know that my father's music is on life support, short term, even at the festivals that were created to preserve it. Did I save his old 78s? What the hell would I play them on? Where the hell are my old jazz LPs? Does my stereo receiver still work? Can I still buy vacuum tubes?

They're starting to stir, draining their wine glasses. They get up. Two of them drop money on the table. The other two;

not her. They do those two-cheek kisses. She sits back down.
Still has a little wine left.

I continue writing, with my head down, but just up enough
to see what she's doing. She lifts her glass, takes a sip, holds it in
front of her for a second and tips it, almost imperceptibly, as
feigning a salute. The wry smile again.

Oh, God!

Deep breath.

Can I get it right this time?

. . .

☘

JUST JOSEPHINE

"Oh come on, Josephine," I said, "you're
my friend."
She put on an exaggerated pout.
"OK, my *best* friend."
"Thanks a lot . . . friend."
We went on dancing.

Josephine Milano and I were both born on August 8, 1941, into
homes on the same block in Astoria, part of New York City's
quintessentially suburban borough of Queens. At my second
birthday party, with Josephine in attendance and celebrating
along with me, I asked my mother if everyone was born on
August 8 each year. Two other girls, Marcia Sanderson and
Jeanette Bruno, who lived on the next street, were born during
that same year but didn't celebrate on August 8. By age three,

having attended numerous toddler birthday parties, I understood humans were being born on days throughout the year.

The four of us shared a childhood together. Our friendships blossomed with the spring and summer months when we were toddlers, playing together in an area that spanned the side-by-side open lots connecting our two streets, an undeveloped green space, where our mothers gravitated, with folding chairs, to catch up on the latest community gossip. This mini explosion in the birthrate during the early '40s was an occurrence not uncommon at the time. With draft-age men either already conscripted and headed off to World War II or in about-to-be status, the intimacies of marriage were even more intense than would otherwise have been the case.

As toddlers, however, the four of us were too young to have any understanding of the anticipatory expressions on the faces of family members opening letters from soldiers, sailors and marines serving in the Pacific or European theatres of the war. The closeness of our four birthdays created a relationship among us that seemed to have existed from the beginning of time. It was as if we had been dropped upon the planet to exist as a foursome. That was kind of the way it was among children during those years in the neighborhoods of Queens. The closeness of child's play preexisted the isolated influences of high tech personal media. My friendship with Josephine, in particular, was especially close. Up until we went our separate ways during our college years, I couldn't remember a time when she was not part of my day.

This was an era when bottles of milk were left in a metal box near the front door by a white-suited milkman, where newspapers were tossed up onto your porch by a kid on a bicycle. The man who sold fresh produce came around the neighborhood with his horse-drawn wagon. When you finally traded the ancient icebox for a refrigerator, you wondered how electricity could keep food cold. After men returned home and went back to work, their paychecks allowed families to avail themselves of new electronic devices, some of whose designs

had been perfected with of the same advancements which had
gone into weaponry and other supplies for the war. The new,
two-ton, floor-model TV, with the tiny black-and-white picture
screen, presented three networks with an array of
entertainment programs, which brought visual media into our
living rooms for the first time. "Long-distance" telephone calls to
a city fifty miles away were now possible, although they were
placed by an operator who took down your number and called
you back with the other party on the line, whence you raced
through what you had to say to each other so as not to run up an
exorbitant telephone charge.

During the time from kindergarten and for a few grades
thereafter, life was largely childhood games. They coalesced
around "cowboys and Indians" for the boys, who were
miraculously transformed into centaur-like creatures, with
human uppers and cowpony lowers, galloping around
pretending to be bronco-busters. The girls -- Josephine and her
contemporaries, Marcia and Jeanette -- played "house," sitting at
miniature tables outfitted to look like those in the kitchens of
their parents' homes. Josephine was the only kid among us who
could smack a buttock in a faux horseback rein-slap and race
around with the boys pretending to be a posse, then sit down to
sip air tea from a plastic cup at a play table with Marcia and
Jeanette.

The four of us went through grade school together during
the prepubescent years when a neighborhood girl could be your
friend with no "exterior motives," as Johnny D categorized it, just
a few years later. Josephine embodied that for me. She could
hold her own with the boys when it came to knowing all the
stats for the baseball players on the great 1950s, Yankees,
Dodgers and Giants teams, which all New Yorkers idolized
within our selective allegiances. She collected the Topps
chewing gum picture cards with the same anticipation as the
rest of us, hoping to open a packet and find a Mickey Mantle,
Jackie Robinson or a Willie Mays. Even into junior high, she was
a decent hitter in choose-up softball games at the schoolyard
and was never chosen last. It was not that she was migrating

away from the now giggly neighborhood girls, but she wasn't flitty flighty like Marcia and Jeanette, when the boys started noticing them in the earliest manifestations of those exteriorly motivated ways Johnny D had alerted us to. I always still thought of Josephine as a pal, just Josephine to us boys, and that was always a good thing.

Josephine seemed to have her unique variations on themes that were otherwise more generally accepted by the rest of us. While most of us reveled in the Sunday afternoon kid shows at the movie theater -- a dozen cartoons, the week's latest Jack Armstrong serial and the high action feature films that dominated the schedule -- Josephine tired of that smorgasbord quickly. She preferred instead to join her parents on Sunday evenings, when the theater featured movies of the 1930s and '40s, many of which would become the classics critics would write about for decades: "Gone with the Wind," "Wuthering Heights," "The Wizard of Oz," and of course, "Casablanca." When she found out that one of the TV network movie programs was going to feature "Casablanca," one afternoon during the summer vacation between junior high and high school, she all but resorted to a headlock to drag me into her family's living room to watch it.

Her timing was better than she had even anticipated. It was the summer when I started feeling a strange pull to write. I would scribble down notes about the goings-on around me, then take those observations to places my mind would have them go, creating my own fictional versions of the world for the novels I felt destined to write or the movies I'd script. To preserve my observations, I'd bought one of those notebooks with the black-and-white-speckled covers, the same ones we used in school. I'd begun writing in it every day, developing an almost obsessive need to comment on almost anything.

"Doesn't it just break your heart, Mikey," Josephine said, when Casablanca was over, "the way Rick convinces Ilsa to go with her husband, when he knows he is letting go of the only woman he will ever love?"

I was scribbling in my notebook, almost disinterestedly.

"Doesn't it?"

"I'm still trying to understand how that ending just seems to hang there," I replied, clearly not yet mature enough to deal with the deep-seated consequences of a sensitive love story.

"What do you mean?" she asked.

"This is the beginning of a beautiful friendship?"

"I still don't follow."

"This what? How does 'this,' whatever 'this' is, become the beginning of a beautiful friendship? I just watched the same movie you did. How does that happen?"

She just smiled and said, "There's a Fred Astaire, Ginger Rogers movie next week. What do you think? I could show you a few dance steps."

I crinkled my brow. "Sorry, just remembered I've got to go shoot some hoops with the boys."

No matter my excuses, real or feigned, Josephine was relentless about forcing me to watch these old movies with her, even musicals, which seemed so dated in my world more and more dominated by the rising raucousness of rock 'n' roll. After a viewing of "Shall We Dance," with Fred Astaire and Ginger Rogers, she insisted upon us trying to learn the steps she'd been practicing with Astaire's singing "Puttin' on the Ritz," which she played on her new portable record player.

After much exacerbation, stepping all over Josephine's feet, I started to get the hang of it. "I guess this will come in handy when I have a girlfriend," I said.

"Hey," she replied, bringing our dance to a sudden halt, "what am *I* chopped liver? Hah, Mikey? Hah!"

"Oh come on, Josephine," I said, "you're my friend."

She put on an exaggerated pout.

"OK, my *best* friend."

"Thanks a lot . . . friend."

We went on dancing.

* * * * *

High school became the venue for clubs, which, for the tough guys among us, sprang from informal gatherings in the schoolyard; for the rest of us, as members of organized athletic teams. Our group was the "Shields," our baseball team in Police Athletic League. We had team jackets in our blue-and-white colors, with our logo of crossed baseball bats, which we had special ordered at the sporting goods store. The girls gathered in social groupings, some of them more organized, with jackets that were more feminine, lighter-weight variations on our bulkier versions. Jeanette, beginning an ascent as one of the school's alpha females, formed a group called the "Jitter Dolls," with her sidekick, Marcia, following dutifully along. But by this point, Josephine didn't seem interested in any of this byplay and devoted her time, instead, to her studies.

My friendship with Josephine always seemed destined to continue as part of the natural order of things. We studied together often, with particular strengths that filled in each other's weaker subjects. I helped her with English essays; she helped me with math problems. I viewed our continuing relationship, as I always had, as a friendship. I had friends like the guys on the Shields, but in retrospect, Josephine was indeed my best friend. It just was what it was.

The two of us separated for the better part of our college years, during which we both did well. I had a scholarship at New York University, where I majored in journalism and was editor of the school newspaper. Josephine was a dean's list student at Boston University. We'd see each other when she came back to Astoria during semester breaks, but those had become more passing acquaintances because our breaks didn't quite match up. In any event, by now I was more distracted by relationships with other young women, at this point hormonally based. I continued to see more of Marcia and Jeanette during this period, because we still lived in the same neighborhood, but those had become simply, "hello, how you doin'" relationships.

*   *   *   *   *

As Marcia and Jeanette matured into young women, they grew prettier, in distinctly different ways. Marcia was a petite, fair-skinned blonde with curves in all the right places; Jeanette a

lithe, willowy brunette, with the light brush of a Latinate
complexion and incongruously skewering midnight brown eyes.
The two childhood friends remained inseparable into young
adulthood. Jeanette drove all major decisions, initially for the
two of them, then for those in a widening circle of friends, first in
middle school and into high school. She'd created the Jitter Dolls
as her answer to the boys clubs' intrinsic expression of male
dominance, expressed in the arrogant way they paraded about
the high school in their club jackets. Marcia just enjoyed being
Marcia. She was perpetually smiling, demonstrating, without
saying so, that she just wanted to enjoy whatever aspects of
living life would permit her to enjoy. She was a comfortable B-
student art major at Queens Community College; Cs in all her
other courses. Her claim to fame, within their social circle, was
her design for the Dolls' logo: a silhouette of a jitter-bugging
couple with musical notes above them. Jeanette was one of the
few female business majors at City College of New York, a
student for whom Bs came easily. She was unwilling to work for
As and suffer the possibility of falling short. Socially, she only
dated other business majors from well-heeled families.

Post college, the two of them became one of the in-crowd
duos at the trendy bars where the younger people congregated:
Marcia's easy-going friendliness and curvaceous body attracting
the attention of would-be macho men; then ego-slicing Jeanette
cutting them down to size with the barest curl at the corner of
her lips; her dark, penetrating eyes freezing their awakening
anatomy's southern zone. These encounters invariably followed
the same central theme. Once Marcia's joyful body language had
its inviting effect, Jeanette would slowly coax the interest in her
direction, counterpointed by her finely tuned indifference.
Suitors invariably left empty-handed.

Jeanette, having settled into her social interaction tactics on
the front lines, worked them into broader strategies beyond the
bar scene, particularly where Marcia was concerned. She
sternly insisted that Marcia play by her rules with young men.
She'd break her loose from anyone who attempted a longer-term
relationship, as if the guy were trying to steal away the obedient

puppy dog she'd used to reel in her last shootdown. But she'd always explain it as the young man not worthy of Marcia's attention.

"I guess Marcia needed someone besides Jeanette to talk to about all this, Mikey, so she reached out to me," Josephine said. We were seated at the local diner, during one of her return visits to Astoria after her graduation from BU, this time to prepare for her permanent move back to Boston and the pursuit of job opportunities. "She said she needed someone with some distance from the war games to render an opinion. Marcia was tiring of the inevitable outcome of Jeanette's skirmishes and had begun to question their point."

"No barroom pickup is getting into *my* pants," Jeanette had said to her. "You won't find a future investment banker in places like that."

"Then why are we there?" Marcia replied.

"Entertainment. Purely entertainment."

Marcia told Jeanette the guy who'd been talking to her at their last soiree *was* a business major -- at Queens College.

"Well, that ain't exactly the MBA program at Harvard now is it?" Jeanette replied.

"I liked him."

"So, you should have given him your number."

"You didn't allow me the time to get that far."

"I'm sorry. I just couldn't waste any more of my time there."

"And so it went," Josephine recounted the conversation for me.

"Somehow life in the neighborhood where the four of us grew up seems like time spent on another planet," I responded.

"It's called maturing, Mikey," she said with a smile.

"I don't know," I answered, matching her smile. "Can we go back to cowboys and Indians?"

"Would be nice," she replied, "but I gotta go. Places to be, people to meet."

I nodded. We drained our cups, stood and headed for the cashier.

The conversation marked the beginning of Marcia's attempt to drift away from Jeanette's control. It gained some impetus when Jimmy Thomas, the Queens College business major Jeanette had been so dismissive about, tracked Marcia down through the art department at her college and managed to get her last name out of them. Then he sent a letter to her college mailbox and asked if he could call her. Marcia, thrilled with this level of special attention, replied to his letter immediately.

"We met for coffee at the diner," she said to Jeanette, unable to sit on her happiness about Jimmy's attention. "He wants to take me dancing. He's very sweet."

"Jesus, Marcia," Jeanette responded, "sweet doesn't cut it. You want a kick-ass guy with a business degree so he can buy you things and take you places."

"I don't know. That's your thing, Jeanette."

"She just hammered away at me, after the two times I let him take me out," Marcia said to Josephine in another of their now ever-more-frequent telephone conversations. "Once he took me to a movie, the other time to a quiet club, where we danced. He's a sweet guy, perish the thought. I liked him, a lot. But Jeanette just kept pushing me to shoot higher. I felt like I had to sneak around with him so she wouldn't find out. Finally, he'd had it with my pushing him away and he stopped calling."

"I'm sorry," Josephine said.

"There was something about Jimmy. He was special. It wasn't about the games me and Jeanette played. It was different when he held me. It was different when we kissed. He was gentle with me. I really felt like I loved him."

"I could tell by the hesitancy in her voice she had to qualify her feelings about love, as if it would display the ultimate weakness to Jeanette."

I guess it was not surprising when their world -- our world -- turned upside down not long after. But none of us could have predicted the tragic outcome of these sparring matches.

*　*　*　*　*

182

"The last time I spoke with Marcia she'd called me just before I headed back to Boston to look for work and a place to live." Josephine and I were standing behind our local funeral home on a hot and humid August night. "There was no mistaking the concern in her voice, Mikey. It was how I found out. Jeanette's influence as her go-to confidant had been waning for some time and it was clear she needed someone to talk to about what had happened."

"You were a non-judgmental neutral party," I offered.

"I guess." She just stood there, staring down at the sidewalk beneath her feet.

"Marcia told me Tim Kavanaugh was Jeanette's most recent castoff when he came to her," she continued. "Ostensibly to plead for her help in getting back into Jeanette's good graces. In a way, Marcia said, she liked the irony of the shoe being on the other foot and her having to deal with one of Jeanette's broken relationships. Clearly, Kavanaugh understood her vulnerabilities, her inherent sweetness. By the end of the night he had forced himself upon her."

"The bastard," I replied. "Her attempts to go her own way had back-fired big time."

"Meanwhile, Jimmy Thomas had recently come quietly back into her life. But she was pregnant. How could she be with Jimmy when she was carrying another man's child?"

"It's heart-breaking."

"One of the girls in Marcia's art class said she knew about a doctor -- in quotes," Josephine replied. "Marcia told me she felt she had no other choice. I could neither discourage nor encourage her. I'm still not sure what I should have said or done."

"Well, we *were* the four musketeers when we were kids," I replied, "but I would never have wanted to provide any advice about that either. With no legal avenue in the case of unwanted pregnancies, how many women have had to suffer the same consequence of our dear, sweet friend?"

"I was reluctant to play amateur analyst to her after a single core course in psyche at BU," Josephine continued. "I felt I could be more useful to just listen. Besides, I had no answer for what she really needed to fix."

"I know."

Josephine just shook her head.

"Well, we know the bastard bragged to his fraternity brothers," I said. "He boasted how it was his way of turning the tables on Jeanette. Then the cowardly son of a bitch ran for the exit when Marcia shared with him the result of his actions and how she needed him to man up. He still insists he wasn't the father, claiming Marcia was sleeping around. The rotten bastard."

We were standing there for a few more moments, with nothing more to say, when the funeral director opened the door and said the service was about to begin. I held the door for Josephine, and we went inside and took our seats. As the priest was about to begin, we heard the back door open and saw Jeanette slip in and take a seat in the back row of chairs.

When the priest had finished and explained the details of the next day's funeral, the attendees broke up into smaller groups. Josephine and I walked to the back of the room where Jeanette was still seated, staring straight ahead, a blank expression on her reddened face and eyes.

"There is no way this story goes this way," she said as we approached and took seats in the row in front of her.

"It was all just a game," she continued. "All part of a game. I guess I knew that. She didn't. God, I loved her. She was my friend. God, I loved her."

"I don't know what to say," was all I could stammer.

"I guess there was a bit of jealousy to it, a contest you had to win. A girl likes to show she is the one who can win the boy, sometimes even if the boy isn't worth the win. Boys, then young men, warmed to Marcia, almost immediately. Life was so joyful for her, and that joyfulness was attractive to boys. At least to the nicer boys. I guess I had to prove how easy it was to pull those guys away."

Jeanette began to cry. "She was my friend, forever. And I enabled her . . . her murder."

"That's way too harsh," Josephine said.

"Had I known about her and Tim Kavanaugh, I would have done everything I could to break them up. I wouldn't even have been subtle about it. He's a bastard. A predator. It was a complete mismatch."

She sat there just slowly shaking her head.

"Marcia viewed that petite, curvy body of hers as a gift from God, to enhance the enjoyment she found in life. It's not that she was slutty or anything, not at all, just unquestioning about the gifts life had provided her. I saw my looks, my intelligence as weapons to use in my war with life. I guess I *was* right about that, and she was a casualty in that war."

Jeanette lowered her eyes, staring down at the floor. Josephine and I were without anything more to say. Jeanette began to cry again.

"The thing is," she said, "I would give any of the victories I have won, or might win, not to be sitting here today. Marcia was my best friend. I loved her in that unequivocal way she looked at life. I was only trying to prepare her for the battles I saw as inevitable."

The three of us grew quiet. Then I rose, Josephine followed, but Jeanette stayed seated. "I need to say my good-byes," she said. "I'd prefer to do it alone."

"Of course," Josephine replied. "Of course," I added.

* * * * *

Josephine and I gravitated back to an apartment I had taken near Astoria Square, not far from where we'd grown up. I felt etherized by the experience of seeing our childhood friend, her lovely, post-childhood looks porcelainized to chalk-white features, frozen in place by the funeral home artists. We'd agreed to try to decompress a bit by spending some of this sorrowful time together, within the comfort zone of our lifelong friendship, with perhaps the only other person who could understand what the previous few hours had taken from us. I'd suggested a drink and perhaps sharing some of the memories of the better times in Astoria among the four of us, to preserve those experiences as replacement for what we'd been forced to endure that day. Josephine said she was staying with a cousin, who lived not far from my place, that she was planning to cab over there. I offered to drive her rather than letting her cab it. I assured her one drink would not alter my ability to get her there in one piece. She accepted my offer.

As I closed the apartment door behind us, I experienced, for the first time with Josephine, a moment of not knowing what to say or do next. For all the times we'd shared as children, at her parents' house or mine, I'd never been alone in a room with her as an adult.

"The drink?" I asked to break the awkwardness of the moment and regain some measure of control.

"Sure," she said. "I was, after all, a sorority sister at BU. I can handle one drink."

It had the effect of eliciting a smile from me, which she returned.

"So," I said, "If we're pretending to share stories of our college experiences, let me say I spent second semester junior year in Dublin, took a side trip to Northern Ireland, where I was introduced to Bushmills and have been a Bushmills neat guy ever since."

"Sounds perfect," she replied.

I reached up to a cabinet over the sink. "Bought this ten-year old version in Belfast. Not sure if it's even available here. I was saving it for someone special. I guess someone like you."

"There ain't no one like me," she said, with an almost coquettish smile.

It was a look I don't recall ever seeing before. At least, I don't think I'd ever seen it. There was no hint of the girlish smile she had shared with me so often when we were growing up together.

I placed the bottle down on the counter and steadied myself against the sink. "Ice?" I asked.

"I thought we'd settled on neat," she replied. "Why would anyone ruin a Bushmills with ice?"

186

"Touché," I answered trying to regain some measure of . . . cool? "I'm starting to feel outgunned here."

We clinked glasses, then spent the next half hour in my living room sipping our drinks, talking about the earliest days in our neighborhood and the fun times with our dearly departed friend.

When we'd each drained our glasses, "I should go, Michael," she said. "I've got an early flight back to Boston tomorrow."

I studied her a moment, perhaps a moment too long.

"What?" she asked.

"When did Mikey become Michael?"

She smiled. "I guess we've grown up."

"Then how come you've always been Josephine."

"Not true. I've always been 'Just Josephine.'"

I had no reply.

" I can't do the funeral," she said. "It would be too painful, shattering memories that no longer represent who we are."

"Understood," I answered. "I'll offer your regrets tomorrow."

"Thank you," she said and stood. She placed her empty glass on my coffee table, anchored there, staring down at it, as if frozen to the spot.

"Marcia was such a sweetheart," she said and began to sob.

"That she was," I replied, placing my glass next to hers.

I took a step, toward her and she folded into my arms.

"Forgive me," she said loosening a bit from our embrace, then wiping her tears with her fingers.

"No need," I replied. "I am as heartbroken as you are."

She looked up into my eyes, her body softening further within the comfort of our embrace. Then, as if by instinct, I kissed her.

"My god," I said, "I'm so sorry."

For a moment, she stared deeper into my eyes, then returned the kiss, pressing her lips more firmly against mine. A shudder ran through me, dissipating as the kiss eased into a soft, brushing touch of our lips. The embrace continued to convey a degree of comfort that fought any attempt I'd make to leave it. It swept through the full length of my body. Then we kissed again, this time more cordially, as if to reestablish the previous kiss as just a kiss among good friends. She separated gently from our embrace.

"I need to go," she said.

"Of course," I answered. "I'll get my car keys."

* * * * *

And so began years of trying to determine what kind of life I needed to carve out for myself, even if that meant an itinerant one, which fed my need to continually explore and discover. Josephine proved the more adept at settling into a life. She'd excelled in math at BU all the way through a doctorate, was hired to teach at the university and eventually tenured. She married one of her former professors, John Hutchinson, a distinguished mathematician whose work made it into academic journals. He was a decade older than she, a widower whose first wife had died young and unexpectantly of aggressive pancreatic cancer. He came to the marriage with a ready-made family of two young daughters. Josephine and John never had children together, but Josephine told me her stepdaughters filled that role lovingly. I got these updates on the chapters in her life when she'd venture to New York from time to time for academic conferences.

My life was more a journey over decades of traveling far and wide, searching for subjects to fill out my need to turn everything I experienced into subject matter in my notebooks. Along the way, I started and ended relationships. Some began with promise but none filling the space I found needed to be filled, the more I failed to fill it. My marriage as a young man was a disaster. My other semi-successful marriage ended in divorce after eleven years, semi-successful because it produced a daughter whose loveliness was for me the keepsake of the marriage. I doted upon her achievements in school, then beyond. The father-daughter love we shared was profound. It only exacerbated the hole in my heart unfulfilled by a lover I could love.

At the core of my problem with women was my inability to understand something represented by what I came to think of as "The Kiss." There were embraces, other kisses, even much more intimate encounters in my life, none of which had ever produced a reaction like that evening after Marcia's wake. All of those subsequent encounters failed to match the reaction I'd had with the woman who had long before secured the position of best friend in my life for my entire life and I knew would hold it forever. And yet "The Kiss" was problematic precisely for that reason. It challenged everything about my history with Josephine, my understanding of the significance of that history. I had always been proud of having a girl for a true friend, with everything that "friend" represented. Until "The Kiss" became a major disruption. Josephine was happily married, with two children she adored. She was living the life she had earned with her dedication to her work, then to her family. There were times when I wanted nothing more than to somehow recreate my days with Josephine, "just Josephine," but her companionship was no longer available to me.

*　*　*　*　*

As the turn of the millennium approached, I used the widely circulating madness attached to the year 2000's Y2K reset of all things computer-connected as an excuse to call Josephine and enquire if there were some kind of mathematical -- even metaphysical -- explanation as to what might happen at the stroke of midnight 2000.

"Really, Michael," she said, "really?"

"OK," I answered, "not really. I haven't seen you in so long and we've not even spoken for some time. I just wanted to talk, or at the very least just to hear your voice."

"I've been planning to call you," she replied, "but wanted to find both the time and the words for what I needed to say."

"It sounds serious," I said, almost flippantly.

"Well," she said, "actually, it is."

"Oh," I replied my tone changing dramatically. "I'm sorry. What is it?"

"John and I are getting a divorce," she said.

"Josephine, I'm so sorry. I had no idea you were unhappy in your marriage."

"The thing is I'm not unhappy. John is a good man, really such a good man. But he's just not my man. I could stay married to him for the rest of my life simply as a convenience or for companionship in the common interests we share. But I ask myself, every day, is this how I want to spend what I hope are the many days until I close out my life? John Hutchinson is a wonderful man, he was a wonderful husband and father, but he was never the man for me, the man who was meant to be."

"I can relate," I said, "for completely different reasons. I've seldom been happy for long in relationships, let alone really sure I've experienced true love. Now I miss what that companionship would mean as I go forward into the autumn of my life."

"There you go," she said, "you who have always been so good with words."

"Again, Josephine, I'm sorry. Where do you go from here?"

"Well, our children are out of college and moving on with their lives. While John did not favor our parting, he too understands the relationship for what it was. We've sold the house, filed for divorce, amicably, and . . ." the ending of her thought just hung there.

"And?" I said, when she offered nothing more.

"I applied for the position of vice chairman in the mathematics department at NYU."

"Here's hoping you get that."

"I've been accepted, Michael."

"Wonderful, I am so pleased for you. You've accomplished so much in your work. It's wonderful to have that rewarded."

"More important than that, I needed to come home."

* * * * * *

One of my editors called with an assignment in Chicago. I remembered my last known contact info for Jeanette was a Chicago address and phone number. The phone number still worked, so we got back in touch. She said she was delighted to hear from me. If I had the time, she insisted upon hosting me for lunch at one of her favorite Chicago restaurants. When I agreed, I was determined to leave any reference to Marcia in the past and just enjoy Jeanette's company. Our conversation began with both of us exchanging pleasantries about where life had taken us, long after the days in the old Astoria neighborhood. She and her husband, William Stewart, had been married for twenty-six years by then and were both very successful in business. He was one of the top traders at the Chicago Mercantile Exchange; she had broken the glass ceiling as a senior vice president at one of the state banks. They owned a duplex apartment in a luxury skyscraper on Lake Shore Drive and a three-bedroom house at a golf community in West Palm Beach, Florida.

Despite my commitment to stay far away from the tragedy of Marcia, when at last the subject came up, it was Jeanette who raised it. It was as if she needed to address it so she could finally put the coda to that part of her life's story.

"You know, Mikey, what saddens me most is Marcia was right and I was wrong," Jeanette said. "And the consequences were so tragic. Things could very well have been different if I had just listened to how she interpreted them, had taken a break from how sure I was that I had things all figured out."

"How so?" I questioned.

"Will and I could lose everything we own, and we would still make it in this world because we were born to be together. I did find my way to him via the path I had chosen. It worked for me. The thing is my path to that end was vastly different from the one Marcia would have led. My problem . . . my fatal mistake was to try to remake Marcia in the way I saw the world. She had found her match in that young man she kept trying to get me to approve of. He was special, she told me. She could feel it, she insisted, she could *feel* it. It wasn't something you could express in words. You just knew it when you felt it. I thought it was her naivete talking. Lo and behold, that is what I felt the moment I met Will. I pushed Marcia away from that special young man, which led to her destruction at the hands of a miserable bastard from my part of the world."

"Even if your methods were not workable in her case, your motives were honorable," I said. It was all I could muster.

She just shook her head, and I could see the tears welling up in her eyes. "Marcia and I were friends for all of her too-short life. I was so wrong, so arrogant to think I could alter her journey in such a profound way. I was never good at owning up to my mistakes. I will carry that sin to my grave."

I told her, once again, she was being too hard upon herself and again stressed that her motives were sincere, the consequence completely unpredictable. She thanked me for my kindness, and we parted company.

The encounter with Jeanette brought perspective to me about the kiss with Josephine. No matter how often I tried to recreate it, sometimes with a woman with whom I had become intimate, passionately intimate, I couldn't make it work. Finally, I connected the uniqueness of the feeling with what Marcia had said to Josephine about the young man who had been so special to her, during one of their last conversations those years ago: "There was something about Jimmy. He was special. It was different when he held me. It was different when we kissed."

* * * * *

On a warm Sunday afternoon in the spring after Y2K had rapidly faded into a non-event, having survived the dud of the predicted computer crash and the earth grinding to a halt, I sat with Josephine in an outdoor café in Greenwich Village, sipping espressos and scarfing down delicious Italian pastries. She had recently relocated to a condominium walking distance from NYU's campus buildings, spread around the perimeter of Washington Square Park.

"You know we're kinda like bookends down here," I said.
"How so?"

"I started my college career here; you've come here to end yours."

"I'm nowhere near the end of mine. Who knows, they say Cal Berkley is looking for a math department chairman."

"Nope."

"Nope?"

"You're not going anywhere. Your passport has been revoked. You said, and I quote: "I needed to come home.""

She smiled that warm smile that had adorned my life for as long as I could remember. "Yes," she said, "home."

I took the last bite of my ridiculously creamy pastry and downed the last threads of my espresso.

"I looked it up," I said.

" What? You looked up what?

"Just."

"just?"

"The adjective, 'just,' as in just Josephine.'"

"And?"

"'Without qualification; absolutely.'"

She smiled, warmly again.

"So, it turns out I knew what the word meant all along. Only I didn't know I knew what I knew."

Her smile warmed further. "And you who were so good with words, now screwing them up."

I returned her smile.

"So," I said, "where to from here?"

"My place for a Bushmills?"

"You have Bushmills?"

"Really? You can ask that?"

"Sorry. No excuse, madam. Shall we?"

I rose from my chair, opened the folder containing the check, fished bills from my wallet and dropped the folder back onto the table.

She rose and held out her hand.

I took it and we began walking toward her condo.

After a few steps, I stopped our progress, raised the hands we held above our heads, twirled her once around and began singing:

"Downtown, uptown get your kicks. Puttin' on the Ritz. Puttin' on the Ritz."

She burst out laughing.

"Damn you and those damned ancient movies you made me watch."

"I like movies. I've always liked movies, especially the old ones. Now that I can record them, I watch the good ones over and over."

"I can understand that."

As we approached her building, she asked, "Have you ever seen Murphy's Romance?"

"Yes, some years ago. Why?"

"The ending. The last line in the movie?"

"Don't remember it."

"Sally Fields asks James Garner, "how do you like your eggs?"

"And?"

"Well," she said, "answer the question."

"Oh?"

She smiled her coquettish smile.

"Over easy."

"That easy, hah?"

I looked at her and smiled.

"*Very* easy."

We entered the lobby of her building.

"You know," I said, "This could be the end of a beautiful friendship."

She turned toward me. "Yes," she replied, "But we will always have Astoria."

". . . as if the connection had just happened in a remnant of the eternal present that was still flickering at your landing here on our planet."

-- Tereza Grymes

EPILOGUE

A CLEAN, WELL-LIGHTED PLACE

'I wouldn't want to be that old. An old man is a nasty thing.'
'This old man is clean. He drinks without spilling.'
                                    Ernest Hemingway

I am following Sophia as she traverses the dining room on her way from the kitchen, heading in the direction of the bar. I have just settled into my seat at my table – *my* seat at *my* table – reserved for my regular, 8 p.m. Tuesday night martini(s) at Norm's Downtown Bar & Grill. Sophia is giving me her squinty-eyed half-smile as she sweeps past my table.

"Take a breath and let it out slowly, old man, don't give yourself a heart attack" she says. "He's already on it."

I nod and smile back.

"That's wise," I reply with my most toothy smile, continuing the word game I play with her name. "Very wise."

She smirks and shakes her head. Sophia is always with the wiseass comments, but I know she loves me.

Mine is a small table, suitable for a single diner or someone who just wants a drink and a bite to eat, away from the regulars at the bar. I've picked the date and the time because it's the slowest night at the bar each week and the dinner crowd begins to thin out. On the wall behind my table is a framed article I wrote about Norm's for the Sunday magazine of the local newspaper. Sophia chides me repeatedly about having written the article just to gain their attention and the special treatment I get. She's right of course. Well at least partly.

I hear the ice crackling against the sides of the martini shaker. I'd been trying not to be too obvious, watching Norm, beginning the process I taught him when I explained my martini would add a touch of sophistication to Tuesday, hump day short one, at his otherwise beer bust bar. (I believe his response was, "whatever.") First he spritzes in a few drops of Angostura bitters, then measures in three jiggers of Martin Miller's, the gin I'd had him stock for me. English gin, of course, but made with Icelandic water, thus raising the bar, at the bar, considerably. (My running bar joke with Norm.) He swirls a coating of Dolin French dry vermouth (bartender me, at it again) in the frosted glass he keeps for me at a secure place in the freezer behind the bar. He drains the Dolin from the glass and pours in the contents from the shaker. Placing the martini glass on a tray, he walks over to me and places it down on my table. A small ritual he created for our Tuesday nights together.

I stare up at him with a puzzled look on my face.

"Whaaat?" he asks.

I nod down at my drink.

He studies it a moment, then, "Damn," he says, "been a rough evening. A lot of pains in the ass." Then shaking his head, "What's one more?"

He sends Sophia over with the olives he'd forgotten, three pitted manzanillas on a toothpick.

"We're too good to you," she says through her half-smile.
"It's because you love me," I reply. "You can't help yourself."
"Calm down, old man. Your heart. Remember?"
"Strong like bool," I say, thumping my chest, then gently grasping the long, thin stem of the glass and taking my first sip. "Poifect."
"Bull, is right," she says, "and plenty of it."
She turns and heads off to make the rounds of her tables.
I take another sip. The smoothness of the experience interposes the slightest buzz –

I heard a fly buzz when I died . . .

There it is again. The interposing fly. I can't turn loose of this: the uncertainty which mortality interposes upon my loosening connection. I reach down into my backpack and retrieve my notebook. I open to the page where I've transcribed the lines by Emily Dickinson:

and then it was there interposed a fly . . .
. . . With Blue - uncertain - stumbling Buzz -
Between the light - and me -
And then the Windows failed - and then
I could not see to see -

. . . and then I could not . . . see . . . to . . . see.

The fading visual here, folks. Where does that take you? I'd started to feel a comfort level with my mortality, but. . .
Say it! With my *dying*.
Some of it is driven by a sense that I no longer belong to a world, which is becoming ever more unfamiliar. I am no longer part of the conversation and have finally accepted I am OK with that. I will leave quietly. But then, there is interposed the lifelong connection to the annoying fly and my need to grip onto the experience of next year's spring, next year's winter snowfall, next year's . . .
While unexpressed explicitly, the subject in Dickinson's poem, after coming to terms with her death, dies in terror when the buzz of the fly reconnects her with the earth's familiar

territory and a lifetime of that experience, just before she falls into the abyss. The black hole to . . .

Will that be the way it is for me? This comfort level with accepting my dying as the transmigration into something better, before the realization – the terror – of finding I'd simply been allotted my time in the best place to be. I'd lived the good life before there is . . .

I take another sip, a healthier one. The effect of the alcohol seems an imperative, driven by the internal narrative.

Is this how the good life ends? Did I *have* a good life? What was there left to do that I'd set out to do? Was I successful at what I'd set out to do? How would I measure that? How do you measure a life?

I take another sip, then pull out the clipping from a Vermont newspaper I'd kept folded inside the back cover of my notebook.

"Area Hotelier Dies After Long Battle With Breast Cancer."

Siobahn Leary had been my benchmark for how to succeed at life. To jump in and make life work for you. But did it really work for her? Again, how do you measure a life? She had said, during that last night at her home in Vermont, the partner she wanted with her as she set out didn't make it onto the LP. Or maybe he was too fucking insecure to not see the connection she had felt. Or couldn't express it. Or maybe . . . it wasn't *his* connection. It wasn't . . . my connection. And what had I done to her . . . done with her?

I drain my drink. I feel this is going too quickly this time, this Tuesday, some sense of necessity at play. I wave my empty glass to catch Norm's eye where he is leaning over the bar and chatting with one of his regular barflies. He sees me and gives me his can't-you-see-I'm-busy gesture. Shaking his head, he motions at Sophia, chatting with two of the regulars, who are into at their coffee-and-dessert course in the dining area, which is thinning out in what's left of the evening. Sophia comes over to my table, swoops up my glass and heads toward the bar. Norm retrieves the shaker and adds a scoopful of ice. He squirts in the drops of bitters, measures in the jiggers of gin, pours a capful of vermouth into my martini glass then sends another of his hard stares in my direction. He does that so I'll turn away and not notice the two jiggers of water he pours into the shaker when he makes my second martini. But it's hard not to notice the additional volume.

Sophia arrives with my drink and a small bowl with an assortment of nuts. Then she heads back to tend to patrons who are calling for their checks and beginning to empty the dining room.

Siobahn? Could she have been the great misconstruct of my life? Had I misunderstood her importance to my existence? How she would always be there, even when she wasn't there? Was she how I had I conflated my first person life with my third person notes to form a narrative with blurred lines? Was Siobahn the opening of a narrative that has since taken me into an exploration through God knows where? I chew on a succession of the bar nuts and take a sip of my martini.

Every time I'm at the local shopping mall, I look for Laura Brennan. I am convinced she will be walking down one of the aisles between the clothing racks, one of those days. I can't help doing this, even though she doesn't live anywhere near here anymore. As if she lives anywhere anymore. She doesn't/hasn't live/lived anywhere ever – *ever.* Anywhere! EVER!

Another sip. Damn watery martini is having its way with me, anyway. Me of the ex-three-martini lunches with my agent, long gone. Long dead. More nuts. Sop up the . . . the watery, watered-down drink.

From time to time, I wonder what Lucy Bartlett thinks of the story I'd written about our time together on the Atlantic crossing. I have no way of knowing if she's ever even read it. How *would* I know if she ever has? We've never had any more contact since the crossing, after I asked her permission to transform her into a fictional character so I could write about our time together. Transformed her from whom? Who was she before? Lucy Blakely? Find & Replace: Bartlett for Blakely. Or was it Blakely for Bartlett?

I chew on more of the bar nuts, take a swallow of my martini. Watered down, definitely. But still having the desired effect.

Aldina has long been the real puzzle. There was/is an Aldina. Of that much I'm sure. The rest of it drifts from fuzzy to opaque. My wife? She's not my wife. Now. Never has been. I don't think. I'd remember having been married and divorced.

I drain my martini, wave the empty glass in the direction of Norm. He pretends he doesn't see me. I give him my teensy-bit-more hand gesture. He continues to ignore me.

I'm having difficulty retrieving thoughts of Aldina. I remember she had that successful acting career on a popular NBC soap opera. I have the newsclip here about her retirement from the show, right here with the one about Siobhan's obit. It's here in the back of my notebook, near the one about Siobahn. The one about Siobahn. The one . . . that one I was referring to earlier. Right here . . . I'll look for it later.

And Gabby? At the hotel in Port au Prince?

And so it goes, time and again. The incurable reflections of Tuesday night at Norm's. Good old Normal. His real name, you know. Abandoned as an infant in Normal, Illinois. So the nuns at the orphanage named him after the city. Or was it a reflection of what they were hoping he would be, one day? At least that's the story he finally fessed up to me. It's here in my notes somewhere? I call him, "Abe Normal." But not to his face. At least I think not. My lids are getting heavy. I squeeze out a few more of the drops in my fight with my martini glass.

. . .

. . . "C'mon, old man."

Sophia is gently tugging at my left arm.

"You've fallen asleep."

My head is upon my arms on my table. I work my brain back to Planet Earth and lift my two-ton head off the table.

"Norm needs to close up. And the rest of us would like to go home to our . . . lives?"

Norm is switching off lights around the restaurant. I can hear the clanging of the kitchen staff finishing their cleanup.

"Sophia will give you a lift home," Norm says as he heads toward the front door to reset the locks. "I'll have one of the waiters drive your car around tomorrow."

"Come on, old man," Sophia says.

Sophia, the Goddess of Wisdom.

"Let me take you home."

Home? Where's home?

"Come, let's go . . ."